Classic
Animal Stories

THE MOST BELOVED CHILDREN'S STORIES

Compiled by Cooper Edens

chronicle books · san francisco

To the memory of Jerry Hall —C. E.

Jerry Hall, he was so small,
A rat could eat him, hat and all.

The publisher gratefully acknowledges permission to reprint the following works:
Excerpt from *The Wind in the Willows*, by Kenneth Grahame. © 1980 Charles Scribners and Sons.
The Runaway Bunny, by Margaret Wise Brown. © 1942 Harper & Row Publishers, Inc.
The Story of Ferdinand, by Munro Leaf. © 1936 Munro Leaf and Robert Lawson.
Copyright renewal 1964 by Munro Leaf and John W. Boyd.
Excerpt from *Winnie-the-Pooh*, by A. A. Milne. © 1920 E. P. Dutton & Co. Inc.
Copyright renewal 1954 by A. A. Milne.
"Blackbird" by John Lennon and Paul McCartney. © 1968 Northern Songs Ltd.
"Octopus's Garden" by Richard Starkey. © 1969 Startling Music Ltd.

Book design by Erik Drohman.
Typeset in Baskerville Old Face.
Manufactured in Hong Kong.

Library of Congress Cataloging-in-Publication Data
Classic animal stories : the most beloved children's stories / compiled by Cooper Edens.
p. cm.
Summary: Stories, folktales, nursery rhymes, and poems featuring animals from Peter Rabbit
and Winnie-the-Pooh to the Owl and the Pussycat and the Billy Goats Gruff, with
illustrations by Arthur Rackham, Walter Crane, and other well-known artists.
ISBN: 978-0-8118-5769-7
1. Animals—Literary collections. [1. Animals—Literary collections.] I. Edens, Cooper. II. Title.
PZ5.C56125 2008
[E]—dc22
2006101771

10 9 8 7 6 5 4 3 2 1

Chronicle Books LLC
680 Second Street, San Francisco, California 94107

www.chroniclekids.com

Preface

I have, for the last three decades, compiled almost annual Classic Illustrated editions for Chronicle Books. *Alice's Adventures in Wonderland*, *Peter Pan*, *A Child's Garden of Verses*, *The Big Book of Little*, *Pinocchio*, *Sea Stories*, *Tales from the Brothers Grimm*, *The Night Before Christmas*, etc, etc. They are illustrated with pictures from old children's books. In my yearly search for images I closely examine hundreds of books, tens of thousands of images. This is a delightful and instructive task, and has led me to several basic conclusions. First, that the years between 1880 and 1935 produced an unbelievably large and excellent body of children's books. Second, that most of the animals illustrated in these books lead delightful existences. *Animal Stories* is the product of this second insight.

What I intend here is a celebration. I hope that my selection and arrangement offer the sympathetic reader the opportunity to waken into one of these animals' fresh mornings, experience a day as one of these enchanted animals, and lay down peacefully under one of these animals' starry nights.

I believe that images are powerful instructors, and that their messages often escape the notice of our rational minds. I strive here to synthesize my complex impressions and believe that a book of few words is the best way to succeed. The reader of this volume should begin at the beginning, step into the dream of each picture, surrender to the whim of each and to the rhythm of one continuous dream.

There is considerable literature on the history of animal-kind. I have for the most part ignored it, for these are not real animals but the animals dreamed by the authors and artists of that time. This is a utopia. It does, of course, have its roots in social reality, but it is reality perfected. The houses and barns and countrysides are rather like this, but here the weather is always pleasant—even the rain is soft. Any fights are clean; any voices raised are sweet. Everything is as it should be. This is a realm of perfection, an ideal never needing achievement, but worth the dreaming.

—Cooper Edens

Table of Contents

Alice's Adventures in Wonderland

(An excerpt)

By Lewis Carroll

Alice was beginning to get very tired of sitting by her sister on the bank, and of having nothing to do: once or twice she had peeped into the book her sister was reading, but it had no pictures or conversations in it, "and where is the use of a book," thought Alice, "without pictures or conversations?" So she was considering in her own mind (as well as she could, for the hot day made her feel very sleepy and stupid), whether the pleasure of making a daisy-chain would be worth the trouble of getting up and picking the daisies, when a white rabbit with pink eyes ran close by her.

There was nothing so very remarkable in that; nor did Alice think it so *very* much out of the way to hear the rabbit say to itself, "Dear, dear! I shall be late!" (when she thought it over afterwards, it occurred to her that she ought to have wondered at this, but at the time it all seemed quite natural); but when the rabbit actually took a watch out of its waistcoat-pocket, looked at it, and then hurried on, Alice started to her feet, for it flashed across her mind that she had never before seen a rabbit with either a waistcoat-pocket, or a watch to take out of it, and, burning with curiosity, she ran across the field after it, and fortunately was just in time to see it pop down a large rabbit-hole under the hedge. In another moment down went Alice after it, never once considering how in the world she was to get out again.

Mary Had a Little Lamb

By Sarah Josepha Hale

Mary had a little lamb,
Its fleece was white as snow,
And everywhere that Mary went
The lamb was sure to go:
It followed her to school one day,
That was against the rule;
It made the children laugh and play
To see a lamb at school.

And so the Teacher turned him out,
But still he lingered near,
And waited patiently about,
Till Mary did appear:
And then he ran to her and laid
His head upon her arm,
As if he said, "I'm not afraid,
You'll save me from all harm."

"What makes the lamb love Mary so?"
The little children cry—
"O Mary loves the lamb, you know,"
The teacher did reply:
"And you each gentle animal
In confidence may bind,
And make them follow at your call,
If you are always kind."

The Hare

By Walter de la Mare

In the black furrow of a field,
I saw an old witch-hare this night;
And she cocked a lissome ear,
And she eyed the moon so bright,
And she nibbled of the green;
And I whispered, "Whsst! witch-hare,"
Away like a ghostie o'er the field
She fled, and left the moonlight there.

My Dog

By Marchette Chute

His nose is short and scrubby;
His ears hang rather low;
And he always brings the stick back,
No matter how far you throw.

He gets spanked rather often
For things he shouldn't do,
Like lying on beds, and barking,
And eating up shoes when they're new.

He always wants to be going
Where he isn't supposed to go.
He tracks up the house when it's snowing—
Oh, puppy, I love you so.

The Rose and the Butterfly

By Aesop

A butterfly once fell in love with a beautiful rose. The rose was not indifferent, for the butterfly's wings were powdered in a charming pattern of gold and silver. And so, when he fluttered near and told how he loved her, she blushed rosily and agreed to be his sweetheart. After a long courtship and many whispered vows of constancy, the butterfly left his beloved. But alas! It was a long time before he came back to her.

"Is this your constancy?" she exclaimed tearfully. "It is ages since you went away, and all the time you have been carrying on with all sorts of flowers. I saw you kiss Miss Geranium, and you fluttered around Miss Mignonette until Honey Bee chased you away. I wish he had stung you!"

"Constancy!" laughed the butterfly. "I had no sooner left you than I saw Zephyr the wind kissing you. You carried on scandalously with Mr. Bumble Bee, and you made eyes at every single bug you could see. You can't expect any constancy from me!"

Do not expect others to be faithful unless you are faithful yourself.

Blackbird

By John Lennon and Paul McCartney

Blackbird singing in the dead of night
Take these broken wings and learn to fly
All your life
You were only waiting for this moment to arise.

Blackbird singing in the dead of night
Take these sunken eyes and learn to see
All your life
You were only waiting for this moment to be free.

Blackbird fly, blackbird fly
Into the light of the dark black night.

Hickory, Dickory, Dock

By Mother Goose

Hickory, dickory, dock,
The mouse ran up the clock;
The clock struck one,
The mouse ran down,
Hickory, dickory, dock.

A Message from the Crane

By Pak Fu-Jin

On a deserted islet in the ocean
Stay even if the sun sets and the moon
Stay even if winds howl and rain

During the day chitchat with waves
At night repeat the names of stars
Memorize the names of countless stars

Eat grass berries
Wet your throat with dewdrops

Weave your dress with flowers
Inscribe your syllables on the sand

Wait there
On that lonely island

Don't say my words are foolish
The words I send to the winds

Flying over the six oceans
I'll bring you back

The joy
Of wings growing from my shoulders
Of my flesh and bones

'Til that day that morning
Wait

Robin Red-Breast

Anonymous

Little Robin Red-Breast
Sat upon a rail:
Niddle-naddle went his head!
Wiggle-waggle went his tail.

Little Robin Red-Breast,
Where do you live?
Up in yon wood, child,
On a hazel twig.

Old MacDonald

Anonymous

Old MacDonald had a farm, E-I-E-I-O
And on this farm he had some chicks, E-I-E-I-O
With a chick, chick here and a chick, chick there
Here a chick, there a chick, everywhere a chick, chick.
Old MacDonald had a farm, E-I-E-I-O

Old MacDonald had a farm, E-I-E-I-O
And on this farm he had some turkeys, E-I-E-I-O
With a gobble, gobble here and a gobble, gobble there
Here a gobble, there a gobble, everywhere a gobble, gobble.
Old MacDonald had a farm, E-I-E-I-O

Old MacDonald had a farm, E-I-E-I-O
And on this farm he had some pigs, E-I-E-I-O
With an oink, oink here and an oink, oink there
Here an oink, there an oink, everywhere an oink, oink.
Old MacDonald had a farm, E-I-E-I-O

Old MacDonald had a farm, E-I-E-I-O
And on this farm he had some cows, E-I-E-I-O
With a moo, moo here and a moo, moo there
Here a moo, there a moo, everywhere a moo, moo.
Old MacDonald had a farm, E-I-E-I-O

Old MacDonald had a farm, E-I-E-I-O
And on this farm he had some donkeys, E-I-E-I-O
With a hee, haw here and a hee, haw there
Here a hee, there a haw, everywhere a hee, haw.
Old MacDonald had a farm, E-I-E-I-O

There'll Be Bluebirds over the White Cliffs of Dover

By Nat Burton and Walter Kent

There'll be bluebirds over the white cliffs of Dover,
Tomorrow, just you wait and see.
There'll be love and laughter and peace ever after,
Tomorrow, when the world is free.
The shepherd will tend his sheep, the valley will bloom again;
And Jimmy will go to sleep, in his own little room again.

Froggie Went a-Courtin'

American Folk Song

Froggie went a-courtin' and he did ride, uh-huh, uh-huh
Froggie went a-courtin' and he did ride
Sword and pistol by his side, uh-huh, uh-huh.

Well, he rode down to Miss Mousie's door
Where he had often been before, uh-huh, uh-huh;
He took Miss Mousie on his knee
Said, "Miss Mousie will you marry me?"

"I'll have to ask my Uncle Rat
See what he will say to that,
Without my Uncle Rat's consent
I would not marry the President."

25

The
Wind
in the Willows

(An excerpt)

By Kenneth Grahame

But what I wanted to ask you was, won't you take me to call on Mr. Toad? I've heard so much about him, and I do so want to make his acquaintance."

"Why, certainly," said the good-natured Rat, jumping to his feet and dismissing poetry from his mind for the day. "Get the boat out, and we'll paddle up there at once. It's never the wrong time to call on Toad. Early or late he's always the same fellow. Always good-tempered, always glad to see you, always sorry when you go!"

"He must be a very nice animal," observed the Mole, as he got into the boat and took the sculls, while the Rat settled himself comfortably in the stern.

"He is indeed the best of animals," replied Rat. "So simple, so good-natured, and so affectionate. Perhaps he's not very clever—we can't all be geniuses; and it may be that he is both boastful and conceited. But he has got some great qualities, has Toady."

Rounding a bend in the river, they came in sight of a handsome, dignified old house of mellowed red brick, with well-kept lawns reaching down to the water's edge.

"There's Toad Hall," said the Rat; "and that creek on the left, where the notice board says 'Private. No landing allowed,' leads to his boathouse, where we'll leave the boat. The stables are over there to the right. That's the banqueting hall you're looking at now—very old, that is. Toad is rather rich, you know, and this is really one of the nicest houses in these parts, though we never admit as much to Toad."

They glided up the creek, and the Mole slipped his sculls as they passed into the shadow of a large boathouse. Here they saw many handsome boats, slung from the crossbeams or hauled up on a slip, but none in the water; and the place had an unused and deserted air.

The Rat looked around him. "I understand," said he. "Boating is played out. He's tired of it and done with it. I wonder what new fad he has taken up now? Come along and let's look him up. We shall hear all about it quite soon enough."

They disembarked and strolled across the gay, flower-decked lawns in search of Toad, whom they presently happened upon resting in a wicker garden chair, with a preoccupied expression of face and a large map spread out on his knees.

"Hooray!" he cried, jumping up on seeing them, "this is splendid!" He shook the paws of both of them warmly, never waiting for an introduction to the Mole. "How *kind* of you!" he went on, dancing round them. "I was just going to send a boat down the river for you, Ratty, with strict orders that you were to be fetched up here at once, whatever you were doing. I want you badly—both of you. Now what will you take? Come inside and have something! You don't know how lucky it is, your turning up just now!"

"Let's sit quiet a bit, Toady!" said the Rat, throwing himself into an easy chair, while the Mole took another by the side of him and made some civil remark about Toad's "delightful residence."

"Finest house on the whole river," cried Toad boisterously. "Or anywhere else, for that matter," he could not help adding.

Here the Rat nudged the Mole. Unfortunately the Toad saw him do it and turned very red. There was a moment's painful silence. Then Toad burst out laughing. "All right, Ratty," he said. "It's only my way, you know. And it's not such a very bad house, is it? You know you rather like it yourself. Now, look here. Let's be sensible. You are the very animals I wanted. You've got to help me. It's most important!"

"It's about your rowing, I suppose," said the Rat, with an innocent air. "You're getting on fairly well, though you splash a good bit still. With a great deal of patience and any quantity of coaching, you may—"

"O, pooh! Boating!" interrupted the Toad, in great disgust. "Silly boyish amusement. I've given that up long ago. Sheer waste of time, that's what it is. It makes me downright sorry to see you fellows, who ought to know better, spending all your energies in that aimless manner. No, I've discovered the real thing, the only genuine occupation for a lifetime. I propose to devote the remainder of mine to it and can only regret the wasted years that lie behind me, squandered in trivialities. Come with me, dear Ratty, and your amiable friend also, if he will be so very good, just as far as the stable yard, and you shall see what you shall see!"

He led the way to the stable yard accordingly, the Rat following with a most mistrustful expression; and there, drawn out of the coach house into the open, they saw a gypsy caravan, shining with newness, painted canary-yellow picked out with green, and red wheels.

"There you are!" cried the Toad, straddling and expanding himself. "There's real life for you, embodied in that little cart. The open road, the dusty highway, the heath, the common, the hedgerows, the rolling downs! Camps, villages, towns, cities! Here today, up and off to somewhere else tomorrow! Travel, change, interest, excitement! The whole world before you and a horizon that's always changing! And mind, this the very finest cart of its sort that was ever built, without any exception. Come inside and look at the arrangements. Planned 'em all myself, I did!"

The Mole was tremendously interested and excited and followed him eagerly up the steps and into the interior of the caravan. The Rat only snorted and thrust his hands deep into his pockets, remaining where he was.

It was indeed very compact and comfortable. Little sleeping bunks—a little table that folded up against the wall—a cooking stove, lockers, bookshelves, a birdcage with a bird in it; and pots, pans, jugs, and kettles of every size and variety.

"All complete!" said the Toad triumphantly, pulling open a locker. "You see—biscuits, potted lobster, sardines—everything you can possibly want. Soda water here—baccy there—letter paper, bacon, jam, cards, and dominoes—" he continued, as they descended the steps again, "you'll find that nothing whatever has been forgotten when we make our start this afternoon."

"I beg your pardon," said the Rat slowly, as he chewed a straw, "but did I overhear you say something about 'we,' and 'start,' and 'this afternoon'?"

"Now, you dear good old Ratty," said Toad imploringly, "don't begin talking in that stiff and sniffy sort of way, because you know you've *got* to come. I can't possibly manage without you, so please consider it settled, and don't argue—it's the one thing I can't stand. You surely don't mean to stick to your dull fusty old river all your life, and just live in a hole in a bank, and boat? I want to show you the world! I'm going to make an *animal* of you, my boy!"

The Ants and the Grasshopper

By Aesop

All summer long, a merry grasshopper spent his days making music. When he saw the ants marching past him in a line, carrying seeds and grain to store in their hill, he laughed at their toil. "How foolish, to work so hard in the hot sun!" the grasshopper cried. "Summer's the time to play and sing. There's time enough to worry about winter when the first snow falls."

But when the days grew short and the first snow fell, the grasshopper could find nothing to eat. Shivering in the cold, he came to ask the ants for help. "Please, can't you spare me a seed or a leaf?" he begged. "I'm too hungry even to sing!"

The ants shrugged in disdain. "We worked hard for our food and we have none to spare," they said. "All summer long you made nothing but music. Now all winter long you can dance!"

Don't put off for tomorrow what you should do today.

The Three Billy Goats Gruff

By The Brothers Grimm

Once upon a time, there were three Billy Goats named Gruff. They loved to go into the green, green pasture to eat the juicy grass. On their way to the pasture they had to cross a bridge.

Under the bridge lived a fearful troll, with eyes as big as saucers and a nose as long as a poker.

One day Little Billy Goat Gruff decided to cross the bridge into the lovely pasture. As he started over the bridge, his little hoofs said, "Trip, trap, trip, trap."

"Who's that tripping over my bridge?" roared the troll.

"It is I, Little Billy Goat Gruff," replied the goat in his little voice.

"I'm coming up to eat you!" roared the troll in a great, deep voice.

"Oh, please don't eat me, Mr. Troll," cried Little Billy Goat Gruff. "Wait until tomorrow. Then my brother will be coming over the bridge. He is bigger than I and will make a much better meal."

"Get along, then," roared the troll, and the little goat tripped on over the bridge to eat the juicy green grass.

The next day Middle-Sized Billy Goat Gruff decided to go to the pasture. As he crossed over the bridge, his hoofs said, "Trip, trap, trip, trap," a little more loudly than his brother's because he was bigger.

"Who's that tripping over my bridge?" roared the troll.

"It is I, Middle-Sized Billy Goat Gruff," replied the goat in his medium-sized voice.

"I'm coming up to get you!" roared the troll.

"Oh, please, Mr. Troll, don't eat me!" said the goat. "Wait until tomorrow. Then my brother will be coming over the bridge. He is bigger than I and will make a much better meal."

"Get along, then," roared the troll, and the goat tripped on over the bridge to eat the juicy green grass.

The next day Big Billy Goat Gruff started over to join his brothers in the pasture. As he started over the bridge, his hoofs said, "TRIP, TRAP, TRIP, TRAP," because he was so big.

"Who's that tripping over my bridge?" roared the troll.

"It is I, Big Billy Goat Gruff," roared back the goat.

"I'm coming up to get you!" boomed the troll.

"Come along, then," boomed back the goat in just as loud a voice.

When the troll, with his eyes as big as saucers and his nose as long as a poker, put his head over the side of the bridge, Big Billy Goat Gruff put down his head and butted that troll over the bridge and into the water, and he was never seen beneath that bridge again.

The three Billy Goats Gruff met together in the pasture, where they ate the delicious grass and became so very fat they could hardly walk back over the bridge to their home.

Old Noah's Ark

Anonymous

Old Noah, once he built an ark,
And patched it up with hickory bark.
He anchored it to a great big rock,
And then he began to load his stock.
The animals went in one by one,
The elephant chewing a caraway bun.
The animals went in two by two,
The crocodile and the kangaroo.
The animals went in three by three,
The tall giraffe and the tiny flea.
The animals went in four by four,
The hippopotamus stuck in the door.
The animals went in five by five,
The bees mistook the bear for a hive.
The animals went in seven by seven,
Said the ant to the elephant, "Who're you
　　shov'n?"
The animals went in eight by eight,
Some were early and some were late.
The animals went in nine by nine,
Said the whale, "Not me, the water's fine,"
The animals went in ten by ten,
If you want any more, you can read it again.

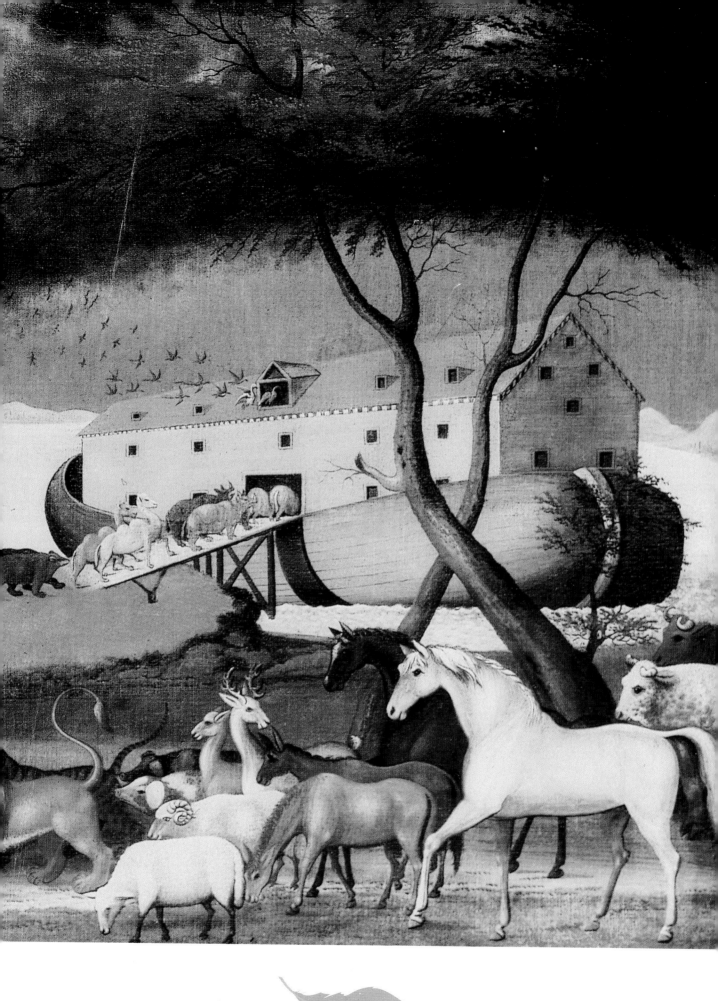

The Raven

(An excerpt)

By Edgar Allan Poe

Once upon a midnight dreary, while I pondered, weak and weary,
Over many a quaint and curious volume of forgotten lore,
While I nodded, nearly napping, suddenly there came a tapping,
As of someone gently rapping, rapping at my chamber door.
"'Tis some visitor," I muttered, "tapping at my chamber door—
Only this and nothing more."

Ah, distinctly I remember, it was in the bleak December,
And each separate dying ember wrought its ghost upon the floor.
Eagerly I wished the morrow—vainly I had sought to borrow
From my books surcease of sorrow—sorrow for the lost Lenore—
For the rare and radiant maiden whom the angels named Lenore—
Nameless here for evermore.

And the silken sad uncertain rustling of each purple curtain
Thrilled me—filled me with fantastic terrors never felt before;
So that now, to still the beating of my heart, I stood repeating
"'Tis some visitor entreating entrance at my chamber door—
Some late visitor entreating entrance at my chamber door—
This it is and nothing more."

Presently my soul grew stronger; hesitating then no longer,
"Sir," said I, "or Madam, truly your forgiveness I implore;
But the fact is I was napping, and so gently you came rapping,
And so faintly you came tapping, tapping at my chamber door,
That I scarce was sure I heard you"—here I opened wide the door—
Darkness there and nothing more.

Back into the chamber turning, all my soul within me burning,
Soon again I heard a tapping, somewhat louder than before.
"Surely," said I, "surely that is something at my window lattice;
Let me see, then, what thereat is, and this mystery explore—
Let my heart be still a moment, and this mystery explore—
'Tis the wind and nothing more!"

Open here I flung the shutter, when, with many a flirt and flutter,
In there stepped a stately Raven of the saintly days of yore.
Not the least obeisance made he; not an instant stopped or stayed he;
But, with mien of lord or lady, perched above my chamber door—
Perched upon a bust of Pallas just above my chamber door—
Perched and sat and nothing more.

Then this ebony bird beguiling my sad fancy into smiling,
By the grave and stern decorum of the countenance it wore,
"Though thy crest be shorn and shaven, thou," I said, "art sure no craven,
Ghastly grim and ancient Raven wandering from the Nightly shore—
Tell me what thy lordly name is on the Night's Plutonian shore!"
Quoth the Raven, "Nevermore."

Then, methought, the air grew denser, perfumed from an unseen censer,
Swung by Seraphim whose footfalls tinkled on the tufted floor.
"Wretch," I cried, "thy God hath lent thee—by these angels he hath sent thee
Respite—respite and nepenthe from thy memories of Lenore!
Quaff, oh quaff this kind nepenthe, and forget this lost Lenore!"
Quoth the Raven, "Nevermore."

"Be that word our sign of parting, bird or fiend!" I shrieked, upstarting—
"Get thee back into the tempest and the Night's Plutonian shore!
Leave no black plume as a token of that lie thy soul hath spoken!
Leave my loneliness unbroken!—quit the bust above my door!
Take thy beak from out my heart, and take thy form from my door!"
Quoth the Raven, "Nevermore."

And the Raven, never flitting, still is sitting, still is sitting
On the pallid bust of Pallas just above my chamber door;
And his eyes have all the seeming of a Demon's that is dreaming,
And the lamplight o'er him streaming throws his shadow on the floor;
And my soul from out that shadow that lies floating on the floor
Shall be lifted—nevermore!

The Lion and the Unicorn

By Mother Goose

The lion and the unicorn
Were fighting for the crown;
The lion beat the unicorn
All 'round the town.

Some gave them white bread
And some gave them the brown;
Some gave them plum-cake
And sent them out of town.

The Three Little Pigs

Anonymous

nce upon a time there was an old pig with three little pigs, and as she had not enough to keep them, she sent them out to seek their fortune.

The first that went off met a man with a bundle of straw and said to him, "Please, man, give me the straw to build me a house," which the man did, and the little pig built a house with it.

Presently came along a wolf and knocked at the door and said, "Little pig, little pig, let me come in!"

To which the pig answered, "No, no, by the hair of my chinny chin chin!"

The wolf then answered to that, "Then I'll huff, and I'll puff, and I'll blow your house in."

So he huffed, and he puffed, and he blew the house in and ate up the little pig.

The second little pig met a man with a bundle of sticks and said, "Please, man, give me those sticks to build a house," which the man did, and the pig built his house.

Then along came the wolf and said, "Little pig, little pig, let me come in!"

"No, no, by the hair of my chinny chin chin!"

"Then I'll huff, and I'll puff, and I'll blow your house in!"

So he huffed, and he puffed, and he puffed, and he huffed, and at last he blew the house down, and he ate up the little pig.

The third little pig met a man with a load of bricks and said, "Please, man, give me those bricks to build a house with"; so the man gave him the bricks, and he built his house with them.

So the wolf came, as he did to the other little pigs, and said, "Little pig, little pig, let me come in!"

"No, no, by the hair of my chinny chin chin!"

"Then I'll huff, and I'll puff, and I'll blow your house in."

Well, he huffed, and he puffed, and he huffed, and he puffed, and he puffed, and he huffed. But he could not, with all his huffing and puffing, blow the house down.

He said, "Little pig, I know where there is a nice field of turnips."

"Where?" said the little pig.

"Oh, in Mrs. Smith's field, and if you will be ready tomorrow morning, I will call for you, and we will go together and get some dinner."

"Very well," said the little pig. "I will be ready. What time do you mean to go?"

"Oh, at six o'clock."

Well, the little pig got up at five and got the turnips before the wolf came (which he did about six) and said, "Little pig, are you ready?"

The little pig replied, "Ready! I have been and come back again, and got a nice potful for dinner."

The wolf felt very angry at this, but thought that he would be up to the little pig somehow or other, so he said, "Little pig, I know where there is a nice apple tree."

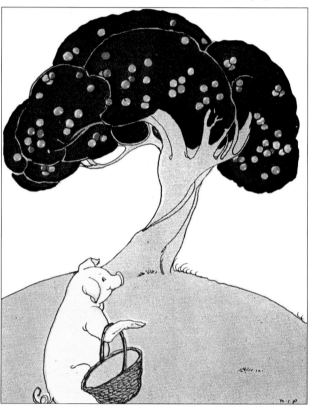

"Where?" said the pig.

"Down at Merry-garden," replied the wolf, "and if you will not deceive me, I will come for you at five o'clock tomorrow, and we will go together and get some apples."

Well, the little pig bustled up the next morning at four o'clock and went off for the apples, hoping to get back before the wolf came; but he had further to go and had to climb the tree, so that just as he was coming down from it, he saw the wolf coming and, as you may suppose, this frightened him very much.

When the wolf came up he said, "Little pig, what are you doing here before me? Are they nice apples?"

"Yes, very," said the little pig. "I will throw you down one," and he threw it so far, that, while the wolf was going to pick it up, the little pig jumped down and ran home.

The next day, the wolf came again and said to the little pig, "Little pig, there is a fair at Shanklin this afternoon; will you go?"

"Oh yes," said the pig, "I will go: what time shall you be ready?"

"At three," said the wolf.

So the little pig went off before the time, as usual, and got to the fair and bought a butter-churn, which he was going home with when he saw the wolf coming. Then he could not tell what to do. So he got into the churn to hide and, by so doing, turned it round, and it rolled down the hill with the pig in it, which frightened the wolf so much that he ran home without going to the fair. He went to the little pig's house and told him how frightened he had been by the great round thing that came down the hill past him.

Then the little pig said, "Ha! I frightened you then. I had been to the fair and bought a butter-churn, and when I saw you, I got into it and rolled down the hill!"

Then the wolf was very angry indeed and declared he would eat up the little pig, and that he would get down the chimney after him.

When the little pig saw what he was about, he hung up the pot full of water and made a blazing fire, and just as the wolf was coming down, took off the cover, and in fell the wolf: so the little pig put on the cover again in an instant, boiled him up, and ate him for supper and lived happy ever afterward.

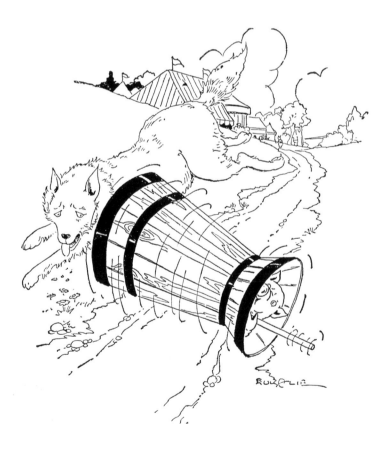

Teddy Bears' Picnic

By Jimmy Kennedy and John W. Bratton

If you go down in the woods today
You're sure of a big surprise
If you go down in the woods today
You'd better go in disguise
For every bear that ever there was
Will gather there for certain because
Today's the day the Teddy bears have their picnic.

Every Teddy bear who's been good
Is sure of a treat today
There're lots of marvelous things to eat
And wonderful games to play
Beneath the trees where nobody sees
They'll hide and seek as long as they please
'Cause that's the way the Teddy bears have their picnic.

If you go down in the woods today
You'd better not go alone
It's lovely down in the woods today
But safer to stay at home
For every bear that ever there was
Will gather there for certain because
Today's the day the Teddy bears have their picnic.

Picnic time for Teddy Bears
The little Teddy bears are having a lovely time today
Watch them, catch them unawares
And see them picnic on their holiday
See them gaily gad about
They love to play and shout, they never have any care
At six o'clock their Mummies and Daddies will take them home to bed
Because they're tired little Teddy bears.

There Was a Crooked Man

By Mother Goose

There was a crooked man, and he went a crooked mile,
He found a crooked sixpence against a crooked stile,
He bought a crooked cat, which caught a crooked mouse,
And they all lived together in a crooked little house.

Turkey in the Straw

Traditional Square-Dance Song

As I was going down the road
With a tired team and a heavy load,
I cracked my whip and the leader sprung;
I says, "Day, day," to the wagon tongue.
Turkey in the straw, haw, haw, haw,
Turkey in the hay, hey, hey, hey,
Roll 'em up and twist 'em up a high tuck-a-haw,
And hit 'em a tune called "Turkey in the Straw"!

Oh, I went out to milk and I didn't know how.
I milked the goat instead of the cow.
A monkey sitting on a pile of straw
A-winking his eye at his mother-in-law.
Turkey in the straw, haw, haw, haw,
Turkey in the hay, hey, hey, hey,
Roll 'em up and twist 'em up a high tuck-a-haw,
And hit 'em a tune called "Turkey in the Straw"!

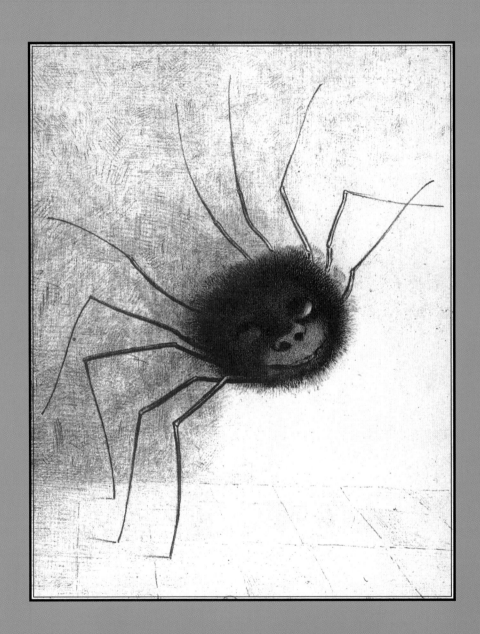

The Spider and the Fly

Anonymous

"Will you walk into my parlor?" said
the spider to the fly;
"'Tis the prettiest little parlor
that ever you did spy.

"The way into my parlor
is up a winding stair;
And I have many curious things
to show you when you are there."

"Oh, no, no," said the little fly;
"to ask me is in vain;
For who goes up your winding stair
can ne'er come down again."

Said the cunning spider to the fly—
"Dear friend, what can I do
To prove the warm affection
I've always felt for you?"

"I thank you, gentle sir," she said,
"for what you're pleased to say,
And bidding you good-morning now,
I'll call another day."

The spider turned him round about
and went into his den,
For well he knew the silly fly
would soon be back again;

So he wove a subtle web
in a little corner sly,
And set his table ready,
to dine upon the fly.

Then he came out to his door again
and merrily did sing,
"Come hither, hither, pretty fly, with
pearl and silver wing."

Alas, alas, how very soon
this silly little fly,
Hearing his wily, flattering words,
came slowly flitting by.

Thinking only of her crested head—
poor foolish thing! At last,
Up jumped the cunning spider and
fiercely held her fast!

He dragged her up his winding stair,
into his dismal den,
Within his little parlor—
but she ne'er came out again!

And now, dear children,
who may this story read,
To idle, silly, flattering words,
I pray you ne'er give heed;

To an evil counselor
close heart and ear and eye
And take a lesson from this tale
of the Spider and the Fly.

The Town Mouse and the Country Mouse

By Aesop

A mouse who lived in the country invited her cousin from the town for dinner. The country mouse worked all day to prepare the dinner, gathering a few peas, a stalk of barley, a crust of bread, and cold water in a green leaf to drink. When the town mouse arrived, the humble country mouse set all the best food before her guest.

The town mouse ate a few of the peas and tasted a bite of the bread, trying her best to be polite. But at last she turned to her cousin and said, "My dear, how can you live like this? Ants and worms eat better food! Come with me to the city, and I'll show you how a mouse should live."

That very night the country mouse went with her cousin to a grand mansion in the heart of the city. The two mice crept into the dining room, where the remains of a banquet were still spread on the table. "Look at all the good things here!" the town mouse said proudly. "Try a little honey on your bread! Have some of the cheese, it's delicious!"

The country mouse gazed about her in wonder. But just as she prepared to take her first bite, there was a hiss and yowl, and a cat leaped onto the table. The two mice fled for their lives and barely managed to dash into a hole in the wall.

"Don't worry," said her cousin. "The cat never stays for long, and we can soon finish our dinner. We'll be perfectly safe as long as the dog stays away."

"A cat and a dog!" cried the astounded country mouse. "My dear cousin, you may stay and enjoy your feast, but I'm going right back home where I can eat my crust of bread in peace."

Poverty in safety is better than riches in peril.

Rabbits

By Zhenya Gay

All kinds of rabbits
Have different habits:
The little ones jump,
The big ones go thump.

Baa, Baa, Black Sheep

By Mother Goose

Baa, baa, Black Sheep,
Have you any wool?
Yes, merry, have I,
Three bags full:

One for my master,
And one for my dame,
And one for the little boy
That lives in the lane!

Zippity Doo-Dah

Anonymous

Mr. Bluebird's on my shoulder
It's the truth—it's actual
Everything is satisfactual
Zippity doo-dah, zippity-ay
Wonderful feeling, wonderful day

Zippity doo-dah, zippity-ay
My, oh my, what a wonderful day
Plenty of sunshine heading my way
Zippity doo-dah, zippity-ay

The Tale of Peter Rabbit

(Escaping from Mr. McGregor's Garden passage)

By Beatrix Potter

Having been warned by his Mother never to go in Mr. McGregor's Garden, that is exactly what Peter chooses to do. Now in danger of being hunted down, he must use all his wits to escape.

Mr. McGregor was on his hands and knees planting out young cabbages, but he jumped up and ran after Peter, waving a rake and calling out, "Stop thief!"

Peter was most dreadfully frightened; he rushed all over the garden, for he had forgotten the way back to the gate. He lost one of his shoes among the cabbages, and the other shoe amongst the potatoes.

After losing them, he ran on four legs and went faster, so that I think he might have got away altogether if he had not unfortunately run into a gooseberry net and got caught by the large buttons on his jacket. It was a blue jacket with brass buttons, quite new.

Peter gave himself up for lost and shed big tears; but his sobs were heard by some friendly sparrows who flew to him in great excitement and implored him to exert himself.

Mr. McGregor came up with a sieve, which he intended to pop upon the top of Peter; but Peter wriggled out just in time, leaving his jacket behind him, and rushed into the toolshed and jumped into a can. It would have been a beautiful thing to hide in, if it had not had so much water in it.

Mr. McGregor was quite sure that Peter was somewhere in the toolshed, perhaps hidden underneath a flowerpot. He began to turn them over carefully, looking under each. Presently Peter sneezed—"Kertyschoo!"

Mr. McGregor was after him in no time and tried to put his foot upon Peter, who jumped out of a window, upsetting three plants. The window was too small for Mr. McGregor, and he was tired of running after Peter. He went back to his work.

Peter sat down to rest; he was out of breath and trembling with fright, and he had not the least idea which way to go. Also he was very damp with sitting in that can.

After a time he began to wander about, going lippity—lippity—not very fast, and looking all around. He found a door in a wall; but it was locked, and there was no room for a fat little rabbit to squeeze underneath.

An old mouse was running in and out over the stone doorstep, carrying peas and beans to her family in the wood. Peter asked her the way to the gate, but she had such a large pea in her mouth that she could not answer. She only shook her head at him. Peter began to cry.

Then he tried to find his way straight across the garden, but he became more and more puzzled. Presently, he came to a pond where Mr. McGregor filled his water-cans. A white cat was staring at some goldfish; she sat very, very still, but now and then the tip of her tail twitched as if it were alive. Peter thought it best to go away without speaking to her; he had heard about cats from his cousin, little Benjamin Bunny.

He went back toward the toolshed, but suddenly, quite close to him, he heard the noise of a hoe—scr-r-ritch, scratch, scratch, scritch. Peter scuttered underneath the bushes.

But presently, as nothing happened, he came out, climbed upon a wheelbarrow, and peeped over. The first thing he saw was Mr. McGregor hoeing onions. His back was turned toward Peter, and beyond him was the gate!

Peter got down very quietly off the wheelbarrow and started running as fast as he could go, along a straight walk behind some black-currant bushes.

Mr. McGregor caught sight of him at the corner, but Peter did not care. He slipped underneath the gate and was safe at last in the wood outside the garden.

Mr. McGregor hung up the little jacket and the shoes for a scarecrow to frighten the blackbirds.

Peter never stopped running or looked behind him till he got home to the big fir-tree.

He was so tired that he flopped down upon the nice soft sand on the floor of the rabbit-hole and shut his eyes. His mother was busy cooking; she wondered what he had done with his clothes. It was the second little jacket and pair of shoes that Peter had lost in a fortnight!

I am sorry to say that Peter was not very well during the evening. His mother put him to bed and made some chamomile tea; and she gave a dose of it to Peter! "One tablespoonful to be taken at bedtime."

But Flopsy, Mopsy, and Cotton-tail had bread and milk and blackberries for supper.

Lassie Come Home

(An excerpt)

By Eric Knight

It was growing dusk as Lassie came down the dusty road. Now she trotted more slowly, and there was indecision in her gait. She halted and then turned back toward the direction from which she had come. She lifted her head, for she was badly puzzled.

Now the pull of the time sense was leaving her. A dog knows nothing of maps and of distances as a man does. By this time Lassie should have met the boy, and they should now be on their way home again—home to eat.

It was time to eat. The years of routine told Lassie that. Back in the kennels there would be a platter of fine beef and meal set before her. But back in the kennel also was a chain that made a dog a prisoner.

Lassie stood in indecision, and then another sense began to waken. It was the homing sense—one of the strongest of all instincts in animals. And home was not the kennel she had left. Home was a cottage where she lay on the rug before the fire, where there was warmth and where voices and hands caressed her. Now that she was lost, that was where she would go.

Lifting her head again, as the desire for her true home woke in her, she scented the breeze as if asking directions. Then, without hesitation, she struck down the road to the south.

Her senses were now aware of a great satisfaction, for there was peace inside her being. She was going home. She was happy.

There was no one to tell her, and no way for her to learn that what she was attempting was almost in the realm of the impossible—that there were hundreds of miles to go over wild land—a journey that would baffle most men going on foot.

A man could buy food on the way, but what coin has a dog to pay for food? No coin except the love of his master. A man can read signs on the road—but a dog must go blindly, on instinct. A man would know how to cross the great lochs that stretch from east to west almost across the entire country, barring the way of any animal going south. And how could a dog know that she was valuable, and that in villages and towns lived hundreds of men of keen eye, who would wish to capture her for that reason?

There were so many things that a dog could not know, but by experience a dog might learn.

Happily Lassie set out. The journey had begun.

The Velveteen Rabbit

(An excerpt)

By Margery Williams

"What is REAL?" asked the Rabbit one day, when they were lying side by side near the nursery fender, before Nana came to tidy the room. "Does it mean having things that buzz inside you and a stick-out handle?"

"Real isn't how you are made," said the Skin Horse. "It's a thing that happens to you. When a child loves you for a long, long, time not just to play with, but REALLY loves you, then you become Real."

"Does it hurt?" asked the Rabbit.

"Sometimes," said the Skin Horse, for he was always truthful. "When you are Real you don't mind being hurt."

"Does it happen all at once, like being wound up," he asked, "or bit by bit?"

"It doesn't happen all at once," said the Skin Horse. "You become. It takes a long time. That's why it doesn't happen often to people who break easily, or have sharp edges, or who have to be carefully kept. Generally, by the time you are Real, most of your hair has been loved off, and your eyes drop out and you get loose in your joints and very shabby. But these things don't matter at all, because once you are Real you can't be ugly, except to people who don't understand."

Dogs

By Ogden Nash

I marvel that such
Small ribs as these
Can cage such vast
Desire to please.

The Little White Duck

By Bernard Zaritzky and Walt Barrows

There's a little white duck sitting in the water
A little white duck doing what he oughter
He took a bite of the lily pad
Flapped his wings and he said, "I'm glad
I'm a little white duck sitting in the water—
Quack! quack! quack!"

There's a little green frog swimming in the water
A little green frog doing what he oughter
He jumped right off the lily pad
That the little duck bit and he said, "I'm glad
I'm a little green frog swimming in the water—
Glug! glug! glug!"

There's a little black bug floating in the water
A little black bug doing what he oughter
He tickled the frog on the lily pad
That the little duck bit and he said, "I'm glad
I'm a little black bug floating in the water—
Buzz! buzz! buzz!"

There's a little red snake playing in the water
A little red snake doing what he oughter
He frightened the duck and the frog so bad
He ate the bug and he said, "I'm glad
I'm a little red snake playing in the water—
Hiss! hiss! hiss!"

Now there's nobody left sitting in the water
Nobody left doing what he oughter
There's nothing left but the lily pad
The duck and the frog ran away—I'm sad
'Cause there's nobody left sitting in the water—
Boo! boo! boo!

The Cunning Crow

(In the style of Aesop)

Anonymous

Once upon a time, a little black crow started out to see the world. He would fly a bit, then swoop down to a meadow and have a nice juicy bug for dinner, and then fly on again. Usually he tried to alight near a brook and take a drink of water after he had feasted.

One day he was so anxious to get on with his travels that he forgot to get a drink at the last brook he passed. He began to fly through a region where it had not rained for a long time and all the streams had dried up. The crow did not know this, of course, and he kept looking down, hoping to see a brook.

"Unless I find water soon," he thought, "I shall die of thirst."

He flew on and on, but looking down so much made him dizzy. He began to fly in circles and finally alighted on the ground. There was plenty of food lying about, but he could not eat because his throat was too dry to swallow.

He walked back and forth, still hunting for water. He became weaker and weaker, but he kept on. When at last he thought he could stand it no longer without a drink, he came to a well. There was a pitcher on the ledge, and when the crow looked inside he saw that it was half filled with water.

He eagerly thrust his bill into the pitcher, expecting to take a long, deep drink. But his bill was not long enough to reach the water.

"I must have this water, or I shall surely die of thirst," he croaked.

In his efforts to reach the water, he almost upset the pitcher, and he felt thirstier than ever.

Now this crow was very smart. He sat down to think and decide what he should do. Suddenly he had an idea. By this time he was so weak he could hardly walk, but he picked up a pebble in his beak and dropped it into the pitcher.

He dropped in another pebble—and another—and another.

Soon the water in the pitcher began to rise a little. The crow thrust in his bill, but the water was still not high enough for him to reach it.

So he brought more pebbles—and more pebbles. The water slowly rose until it came nearly to the top.

The crow put in his beak and drank and drank and drank.

After a while he stopped long enough to eat some of the food scattered about the ground. Then he went back to the pitcher and drank again.

When his thirst was satisfied, the crow spread his wings and flew toward home, where there were cool, clear ponds and swift-flowing brooks.

Soon after he left, a little girl came after her pitcher. She was surprised to find it half full of pebbles, and she never did find out how they got there.

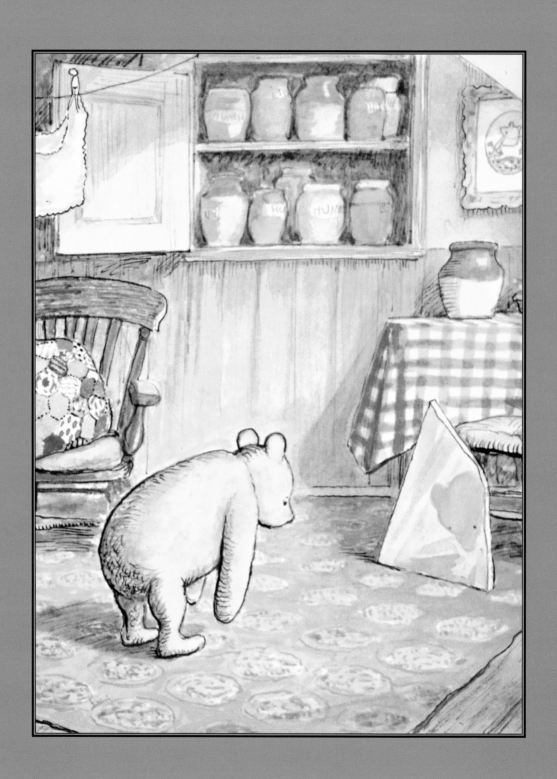

Winnie-the-Pooh

(An excerpt)

By A. A. Milne

Edward Bear, known to his friends as Winnie-the-Pooh, or Pooh for short, was walking through the Forest one day, humming proudly to himself. He had made up a little hum that very morning, as he was doing his Stoutness Exercises in front of the glass: *Tra-la-la, tra-la-la,* as he stretched up as high as he could go, and then *Tra-la-la, tra-la—oh, help!—la,* as he tried to reach his toes. After breakfast he had said it over and over to himself until he had learnt it off by heart, and now he was humming it right through, properly. It went like this:

> *Tra-la-la, tra-la-la,*
> *Tra-la-la, tra-la-la,*
> *Rum-tum-tiddle-um-tum.*
> *Tiddle-iddle, tiddle-iddle,*
> *Tiddle-iddle, tiddle-iddle,*
> *Rum-tum-tum-tiddle-um.*

Well, he was humming this hum to himself and walking along gaily, wondering what everybody else was doing and what it felt like, being somebody else, when suddenly he came to a sandy bank, and in the bank was a large hole.

"Aha!" said Pooh. (*Rum-tum-tiddle-um-tum.*) "If I know anything about anything, that hole means Rabbit," he said, "and Rabbit means Company," he said, "and Company means Food and Listening-to-Me-Humming and such like. *Rum-tum-tum-tiddle-um.*"

So he bent down, put his head into the hole, and called out:

"Is anybody at home?"

There was a sudden scuffling noise from inside the hole, and then silence.

"What I said was, 'Is anybody at home?'" called out Pooh very loudly.

"No!" said a voice; and then added, "You needn't shout so loud. I heard you quite well the first time."

"Bother!" said Pooh. "Isn't there anybody here at all?"

"Nobody."

Winnie-the-Pooh took his head out of the hole and thought for a little, and he thought to himself, "There must be somebody there, because somebody must have said 'Nobody.'" So he put his head back in the hole and said:

"Hallo, Rabbit, isn't that you?"

"No," said Rabbit, in a different sort of voice this time.

"But isn't that Rabbit's voice?"

"I don't think so," said Rabbit. "It isn't meant to be."

"Oh!" said Pooh.

He took his head out of the hole and had another think, and then he put it back and said: "Well, could you very kindly tell me where Rabbit is?"

"He has gone to see his friend Pooh Bear, who is a great friend of his."

"But this is Me!" said Bear, very much surprised.

"What sort of Me?"

"Pooh Bear."

"Are you sure?" said Rabbit, still more surprised.

"Quite, quite sure," said Pooh.

"Oh, well, then, come in."

So Pooh pushed and pushed and pushed his way through the hole, and at last he got in.

"You were quite right," said Rabbit, looking at him all over. "It is you. Glad to see you."

"Who did you think it was?"

"Well, I wasn't sure. You know how it is in the Forest. One can't have anybody coming into one's house. One has to be careful. What about a mouthful of something?"

Pooh always liked a little something at eleven o'clock in the morning, and he was very glad to see Rabbit getting out the plates and mugs; and when Rabbit said, "Honey or condensed milk with your bread?" he was so excited that he said, "Both," and then, so as not to seem greedy, he added, "But don't bother about the bread, please." And for a long time after that he said nothing . . . until at last, humming to himself in a rather sticky voice, he got up, shook Rabbit lovingly by the paw, and said that he must be going on.

"Must you?" said Rabbit politely.

"Well," said Pooh, "I could stay a little longer if it—if you—" and he tried very hard to look in the direction of the larder.

"As a matter of fact," said Rabbit, "I was going out myself directly."

"Oh well, then, I'll be going on. Good-bye."

"Well, good-bye, if you're sure you won't have any more."

"Is there any more?" asked Pooh quickly.

Rabbit took the covers off the dishes and said, no, there wasn't.

"I thought not," said Pooh, nodding to himself. "Well, good-bye. I must be going on."

So he started to climb out of the hole. He pulled with his front paws, and pushed with his back paws, and in a little while his nose was out in the open again . . . and then his ears . . . and then his front paws . . . and then his shoulders . . . and then—

"Oh, help!" said Pooh. "I'd better go back."

"Oh, bother!" said Pooh. "I shall have to go on."

"I can't do either!" said Pooh. "Oh, help and bother!"

Now, by this time Rabbit wanted to go for a walk too, and finding the front door full, he went out by the back door, and came round to Pooh, and looked at him.

"Hallo, are you stuck?" he asked.

"N-no," said Pooh carelessly, "just resting and thinking and humming to myself."

"Here, give us a paw."

Pooh Bear stretched out a paw, and Rabbit pulled and pulled and pulled. . . .

"Ow!" cried Pooh. "You're hurting!"

"The fact is," said Rabbit, "you're stuck."

"It all comes," said Pooh crossly, "of not having front doors big enough."

"It all comes," said Rabbit sternly, "of eating too much. I thought at the time," said Rabbit, "only I didn't like to say anything," said Rabbit, "that one of us was eating too much," said Rabbit, "and I knew it wasn't me," he said. "Well, well, I shall go and fetch Christopher Robin."

Christopher Robin lived at the other end of the Forest, and when he came back with Rabbit and saw the front half of Pooh, he said, "Silly old Bear," in such a loving voice that everybody felt quite hopeful again.

"I was just beginning to think," said Bear, sniffing slightly, "that Rabbit might never be able to use his front door again. And I should hate that," he said.

"So should I," said Rabbit.

"Use his front door again?" said Christopher Robin. "Of course he'll use his front door again."

"Good," said Rabbit.

"If we can't pull you out, Pooh, we might push you back."

Rabbit scratched his whiskers thoughtfully and pointed out that, when once Pooh was pushed back, he was back, and of course nobody was more glad to see Pooh than he was, still there it was, some lived in trees and some lived underground, and—

"You mean I'd never get out?" said Pooh.

"I mean," said Rabbit, "that having got so far, it seems a pity to waste it." Christopher Robin nodded.

"Then there's only one thing to be done," he said. "We shall have to wait for you to get thin again."

"How long does getting thin take?" asked Pooh anxiously.

"About a week, I should think."

"But I can't stay here for a week!"

"You can stay here all right, silly old Bear. It's getting you out which is so difficult."

"We'll read to you," said Rabbit cheerfully. "And I hope it won't snow," he added. "And I say, old fellow, you're taking up a good deal of room in my house—do you mind if I use your back legs as a towel-horse? Because, I mean, there they are—doing nothing—and it would be very convenient just to hang the towels on them."

"A week!" said Pooh gloomily. "What about meals?"

"I'm afraid no meals," said Christopher Robin, "because of getting thin quicker. But we will read to you."

Bear began to sigh, and then found he couldn't because he was so tightly stuck; and a tear rolled down his eye, as he said: "Then would you read a Sustaining Book, such as would help and comfort a Wedged Bear in Great Tightness?"

So for a week Christopher Robin read that sort of book at the North end of Pooh, and Rabbit hung his washing on the South end . . . and in between Bear felt himself getting slenderer and slenderer. And at the end of the week Christopher Robin said, "Now!"

So he took hold of Pooh's front paws, and Rabbit took hold of Christopher Robin, and all Rabbit's friends and relations took hold of Rabbit, and they all pulled together. . . .

And for a long time Pooh only said, "Ow!"

And, "Oh!"

And then, all of a sudden, he said, "Pop!" just as if a cork were coming out of a bottle. And Christopher Robin and Rabbit and all Rabbit's friends and relations went head-over-heels backward . . . and on top of them came Winnie-the-Pooh—free!

So, with a nod of thanks to his friends, he went on with his walk through the Forest, humming proudly to himself. But, Christopher Robin looked after him lovingly and said to himself, "Silly old Bear!"

Piggy and Kitty

Jump-Rope Song

Piggy and Kitty
Dancing in the country and in the city;
Piggy and kitty
Sing *po-po-po.*
Double-dozen and a twitty-twitty.

Three Little Kittens

By Mother Goose

Three little kittens,
They lost their mittens,
And they began to cry,
Oh, mother dear, we sadly fear
Our mittens we have lost.

What! Lost your mittens,
You naughty kittens!
Then you shall have no pie.
Me-ow, me-ow, me-ow.
No you shall have no pie.

The three little kittens,
They found their mittens,
And they began to cry,
Oh, mother dear, see here, see here,
Our mittens we have found.

Wash up your mittens,
You silly kittens,
And you shall have some pie.
Purr-r, purr-r, purr-r,
Oh, let us have some pie.

Old Mother Hubbard

By Mother Goose

Old Mother Hubbard
Went to the cupboard,
To fetch her poor dog a bone;
But when she came there
The cupboard was bare,
And so the poor dog had none.

She went to the barber's
To buy him a wig,
But when she came back
He was dancing a jig.

Fox's Song

By Barbara Angell

Ah bar arkh
a oo ooo a
na-hah na-hah na-hah
err arr arkh!
a oo ooo a

I trot lightly
like new snow
on delicate paws.
Moonsparks kindle
the fire of my pelt.

I sniff earth,
fungus, crumbling wood,
rabbits and small fur,
ruffle of chickens,
taste good blood.

I bark frosty answers
in the wooded night,
flow in and out of trees,
nip stars.

Crows

By Valerie Worth

When the high
Snows lie worn
To rags along
The muddy furrows,

And the frozen
Sky frays, drooping
Gray and sudden
To the ground,

The sleek crows
Appear, flying
Low across the
Threadbare meadow,

To jeer at
Winter's ruin
With their jubilant
Thaw, thaw, thaw!

Ah bar arkh
a oo ooo a
na-hah na-hah na-hah
err arr arkh!
a oo ooo a

The Jungle Book

("Darzee's Chant" sung in honor of Rikki-tikki-tavi)

By Rudyard Kipling

Singer and tailor am I—
Doubled the joys that I know—
Proud of my lilt to the sky,
Proud of the house that I sew—
Over and under, so weave I my music—
So weave I the house that I sew.

Sing to your fledglings again,
Mother, oh lift up your head!
Evil that plagued us is slain,
Death in the garden lies dead.
Terror that hid in the roses is impotent—
Flung on the dunghill and dead!

Who hath delivered us, who?
Tell me his nest and his name.
Rikki, the valiant, the true,
Tikki, with eyeballs of flame,
Rikk-tikki-tikki, the ivory-fanged,
The hunter with eyeballs of flame!

Give him the Thanks of the Birds,
Bowing with tail-feathers spread!
Praise him with nightingale-words—
Nay, I will praise him instead.
Hear! I will sing you the praise
Of the bottle-tailed Rikki,
With eyeballs of red!

(Here Rikki-tikki interrupted, and the rest of the song is lost.)

The Farmer in the Dell

Anonymous

The farmer in the dell,
The farmer in the dell,
High-o! the derry oh,
The farmer in the dell.

The farmer takes a wife,
The farmer takes a wife,
High-o! the derry oh,
The farmer takes a wife.

The wife takes a child,
The wife takes a child,
High-o! the derry oh,
The wife takes a child.

The child takes a dog,
The child takes a dog,
High-o! the derry oh,
The child takes a dog.

The dog takes a cat,
The dog takes a cat,
High-o! the derry oh,
The dog takes a cat.

The cat takes a rat,
The cat takes a rat,
High-o! the derry oh,
The cat takes a rat.

The rat takes the cheese,
The rat takes the cheese,
High-o! the derry oh,
The rat takes the cheese.

The cheese stands alone,
The cheese stands alone,
High-o! the derry oh,
The cheese stands alone.

The Frog and the Ox

By Aesop

Many years ago there was a magnificent ox. One day, when he was taking an afternoon stroll, he attracted the attention of a drably dressed, thoroughly insignificant frog. Staring enviously at the splendid ox, the frog called out to his friends, "Look at the size of this fellow! He cuts a fine figure—but no finer than I could if I tried."

With that he started to puff himself up, and quickly swelled to twice his normal size. "Am I now as big as our friend here?" he asked the other frogs; but they replied that he would have to do a great deal better than that.

The frog puffed himself up some more before asking the same question again. "No," said his friends this time, "and you had better stop trying or you will do yourself an injury."

But the frog was so intent on emulating the ox that he went on puffing and puffing and puffing—till he burst.

Be true to your own character.

Little Miss Muffet

By Mother Goose

Little Miss Muffet
Sat on a tuffet,
Eating her curds and whey;
When down came a spider,
Who sat down beside her,
And frightened Miss Muffet away!

The First Friend

By Rudyard Kipling

When the Man waked up he said,
"What is Wild Dog doing here?"
And the Woman said,
"His name is not Wild Dog any more,
but the First Friend,
because he will be our friend
for always and always and always."

Birds of a Feather

Anonymous

Birds of a feather flock together,
And so will pigs and swine;
Rats and mice will have their choice,
And so will I have mine.

Fuzzy Wuzzy

Anonymous

Fuzzy Wuzzy
was a bear,
Fuzzy Wuzzy
had no hair,
Fuzzy Wuzzy
Wasn't really fuzzy,
wuzzy?

The Old Gray Mare

Anonymous

Oh, the Old Gray Mare,
She ain't what she used to be,
Ain't what she used to be,
Ain't what she used to be,
Oh, the Old Gray Mare,
She ain't what she used to be,
Many long years ago.
Many long years ago,
Many long years ago.

The Goose That Laid the Golden Eggs

By Aesop

Once there was a poor farmer who welcomed any creatures that strayed onto his land. One day a strange new goose appeared among his birds; and when he and his wife came to feed her the next morning, they were amazed to find a gleaming golden egg in her nest of straw. Every morning after that it was the same: the goose laid another egg of solid gold.

Soon the farmer and his wife were richer than they had ever dreamed of being. But still they wanted more.

"One egg a day isn't nearly enough," the farmer complained.

"If we cut that goose open, we'll get all the eggs at once!" his wife declared.

But when they had killed the goose, they found not one egg inside her. "What have we done?" the farmer's wife mourned. "Once we dressed in silks and velvets and ate fine food off silver plates, but now we're just poor farmers again."

Those who want everything may end up with nothing.

Puss in Boots

By Charles Perrault

There was a miller who left no more estate to the three sons he had than his mill, his ass, and his Cat. The partition was soon made. Neither scrivener nor attorney was sent for. They would soon have eaten up all the poor patrimony. The eldest had the mill, the second the ass, and the youngest nothing but the Cat. The poor young fellow was quite comfortless at having so poor a lot.

"My brothers," said he, "may get their living handsomely enough by joining their stocks together; but for my part, when I have eaten up my Cat, and made me a muff of his skin, I must die of hunger."

The Cat, who heard all this, but made as if he did not, said to him with a grave and serious air: "Do not thus afflict yourself, my good master. You have nothing else to do but to give me a bag and get a pair of boots made for me that I may scamper through the dirt and the brambles, and you shall see that you have not so bad a portion in me as you imagine."

The Cat's master did not build very much upon what he said. He had often seen him play a great many cunning tricks to catch rats and mice, as when he used to hang by the heels or hide himself in the meal and make as if he were dead; so that he did not altogether despair of his affording him some help in his miserable condition.

When the Cat had what he asked for, he booted himself very gallantly, and putting his bag about his neck, he held the strings of it in his two fore-paws and went into a warren where there was a great abundance of rabbits. He put bran and sow-thistle into his bag, and stretching out at length, as if he had been dead, he waited for some young rabbits, not yet acquainted with the deceits of the world, to come and rummage his bag for what he had put into it.

Scarce was he lain down but he had what he wanted. A rash and foolish young rabbit jumped into his bag, and Monsieur Puss, immediately drawing close the strings, took and killed him without pity. Proud of his prey, he went with it to the palace and asked to speak with His Majesty. He was shown upstairs into the King's apartment and, making a low reverence, said to him: "I have brought you, sir, a rabbit of the warren, which my noble lord the Marquis of Carabas" (for that was the title which Puss was pleased to give his master), "has commanded me to present to Your Majesty from him."

"Tell thy master," said the King, "that I thank him and that he does me a great deal of pleasure."

Another time he went and hid himself among some standing corn, holding still his bag open, and when a brace of partridges ran into it, he drew the strings and so caught them both. He went and made a present of these to the King, as he had done before of the rabbit, which he took in the warren. The King, in like manner, received the partridges with great pleasure and ordered him some money for drink.

The Cat continued for two or three months thus to carry His Majesty, from time to time, game of his master's taking. One day in particular, when he knew for certain that the King would be taking air along the riverside with his daughter, the most beautiful Princess in the world, he said to his master: "If you will follow my advice your fortune is made. You have nothing else to do but go and wash yourself in the river, in that part I shall show you, and leave the rest to me."

The Marquis of Carabas did what the Cat advised him to, without knowing why or wherefore. While he was washing, the King passed by, and the Cat began to cry out: "Help! help! My Lord Marquis of Carabas is going to be drowned."

At this noise the King put his head out of the coach-window, and, finding it was the Cat who had so often brought him such good game, he commanded his guards to run immediately to the assistance of his Lordship the Marquis of Carabas. While they were drawing the poor Marquis out of the river, the Cat came up to the coach and told the King that, while his master was washing, there came by some rogues, who went off with his clothes, though he had cried out: "Thieves! thieves!" several times, as loud as he could.

This cunning Cat had hidden the clothes under a great stone. The King immediately commanded the officers of his wardrobe to run and fetch one of his best suits for the Lord Marquis of Carabas.

The King received him very courteously, and as the fine clothes he had given him set off his good mien (for he was well made and very handsome in his person), the King's daughter took a secret inclination to him, and the Marquis of Carabas had no sooner cast two or three respectful and somewhat tender glances but she fell in love

with him to distraction. The King asked him to come into the coach and take part of the airing. The Cat, quite overjoyed to see his project begin to succeed, marched on before, and, meeting with some countrymen who were mowing a meadow, he said to them: "Good people, you who are mowing, if you do not tell the King that the meadow you mow belongs to my Lord Marquis of Carabas, you shall be chopped as small as herbs for the pot."

The King did not fail asking of the mowers to whom the meadow they were mowing belonged.

"To my Lord Marquis of Carabas," answered they altogether, for the Cat's threats had made them terribly afraid.

"You see, sir," said the Marquis, "this is a meadow which never fails to yield a plentiful harvest every year."

The master Cat, who went still on before, met with some reapers and said to them: "Good people, you who are reaping, if you do not tell the King that all this corn belongs to the Marquis of Carabas, you shall be chopped as small as herbs for the pot."

The King, who passed by a moment after, would needs know to whom all that corn, which he then saw, did belong.

"To my Lord Marquis of Carabas," replied the reapers, and the King was very well pleased with it, as well as the Marquis, whom he congratulated thereupon. The master Cat, who went always before, said the same words to all he met, and the King was astonished at the vast estates of Lord Marquis of Carabas.

Monsieur Puss came at last to a stately castle, the master of which was an ogre, the richest had ever been known; for all the lands which the King had then gone over belonged to this castle. The Cat, who had taken care to inform himself who this ogre was and what he could do, asked to speak with him, saying he could not pass so near his castle without having the honor of paying his respects to him.

The ogre received him as civilly as an ogre could do, and made him sit down.

"I have been assured," said the Cat, "that you have the gift of being able to change yourself into all sorts of creatures you have a mind to; you can, for example, transform yourself into a lion, or elephant, and the like."

"That is true," answered the ogre very briskly; "and to convince you, you shall see me now become a lion."

Puss was so sadly terrified at the sight of a lion so near him that he immediately got into the gutter, not without an abundance of trouble and danger, because of his boots, which were of no use at all to him in walking upon the tiles. A little while after, when Puss saw that the ogre had resumed his natural form, he came down and owned he had been very much frightened.

"I have been, moreover, informed," said the Cat, "but I know not how to believe it, that you have also the power to take on the shape of the smallest animals; for example, to change yourself into a rat or a mouse; but I must own to you I take this to be impossible."

"Impossible!" cried the ogre; "you shall see that presently."

And at the same time he changed himself into a mouse and began to run about the floor. Puss no sooner perceived this but he fell upon him and ate him up.

Meanwhile the King, who saw, as he passed, this fine castle of the ogre's, had a mind to go into it. Puss, who heard the noise of His Majesty's coach running over the drawbridge, ran out and said to the King: "Your Majesty is welcome to this castle of my Lord Marquis of Carabas."

"What! My Lord Marquis," cried the King, "and does this castle also belong to you? There can be nothing finer than this court and all the stately buildings which surround it; let us go into it, if you please."

The Marquis gave his hand to the Princess and followed the King, who went first. They passed into a spacious hall, where they found a magnificent collation, which the ogre had prepared for his friends, who were that very day to visit him but dared not to enter, knowing the King was there. His Majesty was perfectly charmed with the good qualities of my Lord Marquis of Carabas, as was his daughter, who had fallen violently in love with him, and, seeing the vast estate he possessed, said to him after having drunk five or six glasses: "It will be owing to yourself only, my Lord Marquis, if you are not my son-in-law."

The Marquis, making several low bows, accepted the honor, which His Majesty conferred upon him, and forthwith, that very same day, married the Princess.

Puss became a great lord and never ran after mice any more but only for his diversion.

Bee! I'm Expecting You!

By Emily Dickinson

Bee! I'm expecting you!
Was saying Yesterday
To Somebody you know
That you were due—

The Frogs got Home last Week—
Are settled, and at work—
Birds, mostly back—
The Clover warm and thick—

You'll get my Letter by
The seventeenth; Reply
Or better, be with me—
Yours, Fly.

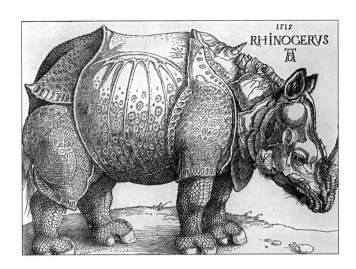

My Rhinoceros

By Edward Lipton

My rhinoceros is silly, when we go for an auto ride
If he doesn't want to go with us, he runs to his room and hides.
My rhinoceros, my rhinoceros, has such a beautiful smile
My rhinoceros, my rhinoceros, but he smiles only once in a while.

My rhinoceros loves donuts, he eats them night and morn
But he doesn't have any pockets, so he carries them on his horn.
My rhinoceros, my rhinoceros, has such a beautiful smile
My rhinoceros, my rhinoceros, but he smiles only once in a while.

My rhinoceros gets dirty and Mama tells him to scrub
But there is no room for water when he gets in the tub.
My rhinoceros, my rhinoceros, has such a beautiful smile
My rhinoceros, my rhinoceros, but he smiles only once in a while.

My rhinoceros gets tired and he has to take him a nap
But you have to tell him a story and let him sit on your lap.
My rhinoceros, my rhinoceros, has such a beautiful smile
My rhinoceros, my rhinoceros, but he smiles only once in a while.

My rhinoceros gets happy, he likes to dance all day
When he's dancing around his room, it's best to keep out of his way.
My rhinoceros, my rhinoceros, has such a beautiful smile
My rhinoceros, my rhinoceros, but he smiles only once in a while.

Peter Cottontail

By Steve Nelson and Jack Rollins

Here Comes Peter Cottontail,
Hoppin' down the bunny trail,
Hippity, hoppity,
Easter's on its way.

Bringin' every girl and boy baskets full of Easter joy,
Things to make your Easter bright and gay.
He's got jelly beans for Tommy,
Colored eggs for sister Sue,
There's an orchid for your Mommy
And an Easter bonnet, too.

Oh! here comes Peter Cottontail,
Hoppin' down the bunny trail,
Hippity, hoppity,
Happy Easter day.

This Little Pig

By Mother Goose

This little pig went to market;
This little pig stayed home;
This little pig had roast beef;
This little pig had none;
This little pig cried, "Wee, wee, wee!"
all the way home.

Wood-Chuck

Anonymous

How much wood would a woodchuck chuck
If a woodchuck could chuck wood?
He would chuck as much wood as a woodchuck would chuck
If a woodchuck could chuck wood.

Hey, Diddle Diddle

By Mother Goose

Hey, diddle diddle, the cat and the fiddle,
The cow jumped over the moon;
The little dog laughed to see such sport,
While the dish ran away with the spoon.

Tell Me, O Swan

By Kabir

Tell me, O Swan, your ancient tale.
From what land do you come, O Swan?
To what shore will you fly?
Where would you take your rest,
O Swan, and what do you seek?

Even this morning, O swan, awake,
Arise, follow me!
There is a land where no doubt nor
Sorrow have rule: where the terror
Of Death is no more.

There the woods of springs are a-bloom,
And the fragrant scent "He is I"
Is born on the wind:
There the bee of the heart is deeply
Immersed, and desires no other joy.

The Little Red Hen

Anonymous

A pig, a cat, and a mouse went to live with the little red hen in her neat little white house on a hill. One day the little red hen found a few grains of wheat, and she decided to plant it.

"Who will help me plant this wheat?" she asked her friends, the pig, the cat, and the mouse.

"Not I," said the pig.

"Not I," said the cat.

"Not I," said the mouse.

"Then I'll do it myself," said the little red hen. And she did.

One morning the little red hen saw that the green wheat had sprouted.

"Oh, come and see the green wheat growing!" she called to her chicks. All summer the wheat grew taller and taller. It turned from green to gold, and at last it was time for the wheat to be harvested.

"Who will harvest this wheat?" she asked her friends, the pig, the cat, and the mouse.

"Not I," said the pig.

"Not I," said the cat.

"Not I," said the mouse.

"Then I'll do it myself," said the little red hen. And she did.

At last the wheat was all cut down, and it was time for it to be threshed.

"Who will thresh this wheat?" she asked her friends, the pig, the cat, and the mouse.

"Not I," said the pig.

"Not I," said the cat.

"Not I," said the mouse.

"Then I'll do it myself," said the little red hen. And she did.

At last the wheat was threshed, and the little red hen poured the golden grains into a large sack, ready to take to the mill to be ground into flour.

The next morning the little red hen asked her friends, the pig, the cat, and the mouse: "Who will take this wheat to the mill to be ground into flour?"

"Not I," said the pig.

"Not I," said the cat.

"Not I," said the mouse.

"Then I'll do it myself," said the little red hen. And she did.

The next day the little red hen asked her friends, the pig, the cat, and the mouse: "Who will bake this flour into a lovely loaf of bread?"

"Not I," said the pig.

"Not I," said the cat.

"Not I," said the mouse.

"Then I'll do it myself," said the little red hen. And she did.

While the bread was baking it smelled so good that the pig, the cat, and the mouse came and stood at the kitchen door. They watched hungrily while the little red hen lifted several loaves, each as brown as a nut, from the oven.

"Who will help me eat this lovely bread?"

"I will!" said the pig.

"I will!" said the cat.

"I will!" said the mouse.

"Oh, no you won't!" said the little red hen. "I found the wheat and I planted it. I watched the wheat grow, and when it was time I harvested it and threshed it and took it to the mill to be ground into flour, and at last I've baked these lovely loaves of bread.

"Now," said the little red hen, "I'm going to eat them myself."

And she did!

A Monkey for Tea

By John Heard

One day I decided to have a monkey over for tea.
I don't know ever why, it just simply did appeal to me.
Of course, the little monkey he did burp ever so loudly.
"Why my gosh," the monkey sighed. "You will have to please excuse me."

The Elephant's Trunk

By Alice Wilkins

The elephant always carries his trunk,
I couldn't do that with my own.
His trunk is part of himself, you see—
It's part of his head—it's grown!

The Hare and the Tortoise

By Aesop

A conceited hare boasted about her speed to everyone who would listen. "Not even the North Wind is as fast as I am!" she declared. "No animal in the forest could beat me in a race!"

Now, a tortoise nearby grew tired of such bragging. "We've all heard you talk, but we've never seen you run," she said. "Why don't you race with me, and then we'll see who is the fastest."

The hare burst out laughing. "I could beat you standing still!" she exclaimed. But she agreed that they would race to an oak tree around a bend in the road. In an instant they were off—the hare soon out of sight, the tortoise plodding step by patient step.

"I've practically won already!" thought the hare as she dashed around the bend in the road. "I could stretch out here and take a little rest, and still beat that tortoise by a mile." And she settled down by the side of the road. She planned to jump up and finish the race the minute she saw the tortoise. But the grass was so soft and the sun was so warm that before the hare realized it, she had fallen fast asleep.

Meanwhile, the tortoise continued on. Slowly she came around the bend in the road and passed the sleeping hare. She was only a few feet from the oak tree when the hare woke from her nap.

Seeing the tortoise so close to the finish, the hare leaped up and tore along the road as if the hounds were after her. But she was too late. Before she could reach the oak tree, the tortoise had already been declared winner by the crowd of cheering bystanders.

Slow and steady wins the race.

Pop Goes the Weasel

Anonymous

All around the cobbler's bench,
The monkey chased the weasel;
The monkey thought 'twas all in fun.
Pop! goes the weasel.

Babe's Barn

By Harold W. Felton

The blue ox grew so fast that Paul
Did not know what to do;
For every time he turned around,
Babe grew a foot or two.

One day Paul built the biggest barn
In all the countryside.
Babe rolled her eyes and licked Paul's neck
And proudly walked inside.

When morning came, Paul found the barn
Perched 'way up on Babe's back.
Babe went on growing all night long
And had outgrown the shack.

The Story of Ferdinand

By Munro Leaf

Once upon a time in Spain, there was a little bull and his name was Ferdinand.

All the other little bulls he lived with would run and jump and butt their heads together, but not Ferdinand. He liked to sit just quietly and smell the flowers. He had a favorite spot out in the pasture under a cork tree. It was his favorite tree and he would sit in its shade all day and smell the flowers.

Sometimes his mother, who was a cow, would worry about him. She was afraid he would be lonesome all by himself. "Why don't you run and play with the other little bulls and skip and butt your head?" she would say. But Ferdinand would shake his head. "I like it better here where I can sit just quietly and smell the flowers." His mother saw that he was not lonesome, and because she was an understanding mother, even though she was a cow, she let him just sit there and be happy.

As the years went by Ferdinand grew and grew until he was very big and strong. All the other bulls who had grown up with him in the same pasture would fight each other all day. They would butt each other and stick each other with their horns. What they wanted most of all was to be picked to fight at the bullfights in Madrid. But not Ferdinand—he still liked to sit just quietly under the cork tree and smell the flowers.

One day five men came in very funny hats to pick the biggest, fastest, roughest bull to fight in the bullfights in Madrid. All the other bulls ran around snorting and butting, leaping and jumping so the men would think that they were very, very, very, strong and fierce and pick them.

Ferdinand knew that they wouldn't pick him and he didn't care. So he went out to his favorite cork tree to sit down. He didn't look where he was sitting and instead of sitting on the nice cool grass in the shade he sat on a bumblebee. Well, if you were a bumblebee and a bull sat on you what would you do? You would sting him. And that is just what this bee did to Ferdinand.

Wow! Did it hurt! Ferdinand jumped up with a snort. He ran around puffing and snorting, butting and pawing the ground as if he were crazy. The five men saw him and they all shouted with joy. Here was the largest and fiercest bull of all. Just the one for the bullfights in Madrid! So they took him away for the bullfight day in a cart.

What a day it was! Flags were flying, bands were playing . . . and all the lovely ladies had flowers in their hair. They had a parade into the bull ring. First came the Banderilleros with long sharp pins with ribbons on them to stick in the bull and make him mad. Next came the Picadores who rode skinny horses and they had long spears to stick in the bull and make him madder. Then came the Matador, the proudest of all—he thought he was very handsome and bowed to the ladies. He had a red cape and a sword and was supposed to stick the bull last of all.

Then came the bull, and you know who that was don't you?—Ferdinand. They called him Ferdinand the Fierce and all the Banderilleros were afraid of him and the Picadores were afraid of him and the Matador was scared stiff.

Ferdinand ran to the middle of the ring and everyone shouted and clapped because they thought he was going to fight fiercely and butt and snort and stick his horns around. But not Ferdinand. When he got to the middle of the ring he saw the flowers in all the lovely ladies' hair and he just sat down quietly and smelled.

He wouldn't fight and be fierce no matter what they did. He just sat and smelled. And the Banderilleros were mad and the Picadores were madder and the Matador was so mad he cried because he couldn't show off with his cape and sword. So they had to take Ferdinand home.

And for all I know he is sitting there still, under his favorite cork tree, smelling the flowers just quietly.

He is very happy.

All the Pretty Little Horses

Anonymous

Hush-a-bye, don't you cry, go to sleep-y little baby
When you wake you shall have all the pretty little horses
Blacks and bays, dapples and grays, coach and six little horses.

Home on the Range

By Brewster Higley and Dan Kelly

Oh give me a home where the buffalo roam,
Where the deer and the antelope play,
Where seldom is heard a discouraging word,
And the skies are not cloudy all day.

How often at night when the heavens are bright
With the light from the glittering stars,
Have I stood here amazed and asked as I gazed
If their glory exceeds that of ours.

Home, home on the range,
Where the deer and the antelope play,
Where seldom is heard a discouraging word,
And the skies are not cloudy all day.

The Frog Prince

By The Brothers Grimm

One fine evening, a young princess sat by the side of a cool spring of water. She had a golden ball in her hand, and she amused herself by tossing it into the air and catching it as it fell. After a time she threw it up so high that when she stretched out her hand to catch it, the ball bounded away and rolled along, till at last it fell into the spring.

The princess looked into the spring, but it was deep, so deep that she could not see the bottom of it. Then she began to cry and said, "Alas! If I could only get my ball again, I would give all my fine clothes and jewels and everything that I have in the world."

While she was crying, a frog poked its head out of the water and said, "Princess, why do you weep so bitterly?"

"Alas!" said she. "What can you do for me, you ugly frog? My golden ball has fallen into the spring."

The frog said, "I want not your pearls and jewels and fine clothes, but if you will love me and let me live with you and eat from your little golden plate and sleep upon your little bed, I will bring you your ball."

"What nonsense!" thought the princess. "He can never get out of the spring. However, he may be able to get my ball for me, and therefore I will promise him what he asks." So she said to the frog, "If you will bring me my ball, I promise to do all you ask." Then the frog dove deep under the water.

After a little while, he came up again with the ball in his mouth. As soon as the young princess saw her ball, she ran to pick it up and was so overjoyed to have it in her hand again that she never even thought of the frog but ran home with the ball as fast as she could. The frog called after her, "Stay, Princess, and take me with you as you promised." But the princess did not stop to hear a word.

The next day, just as the princess had sat down to dinner, she heard a strange noise, *tap-tap-tap*, as if someone were coming up the marble staircase. Then something knocked gently at the door.

The princess ran to the door and opened it, and there she saw the frog. She was terribly frightened, and, shutting the door as fast as she could, she returned to her seat. The king, her father, asked her what had frightened her. "There is a nasty frog at the door," she said, "who lifted my ball out of the spring yesterday. I promised him that he should live with me here, thinking that he could never get out of the spring, but there he is at the door and wants to come in!" While she was speaking, the frog knocked again at the door.

The king said to the young princess, "As you have made a promise, you must keep it. Go and let him in." She did so, and the frog hopped into the room and came up close to the table.

"Pray lift me upon a chair," said he to the princess, "and let me sit next to you." As soon as she had done this, the frog said, "Put your plate closer to me that I may eat out of it." This she did, and when he had eaten as much as he could, he said, "Now I am tired. Carry me upstairs and put me into your little bed." So the princess took him up in her hand and put him upon the pillow of her own little bed, where he slept all night long.

As soon as it was light, he jumped up, hopped downstairs, and went out of the house. "Now," thought the princess, "he is gone, and I shall be troubled with him no more."

But she was mistaken, for when night came again, she heard the same tapping at

the door. When she opened it, the frog came in and slept upon her pillow as before until morning. The third night he did the same, but when the princess awoke the following morning, she was astonished to see, instead of a frog, a handsome prince standing at the head of her bed.

He told her that he had been enchanted by an evil fairy who had changed him into a frog, and he would have had to remain a frog unless a princess should take him out of the spring and let him sleep upon her bed for three nights.

"You have broken this cruel charm," said the prince, "and now I have nothing to wish for but that you should go with me into my father's kingdom, where I will marry you and love you as long as I live."

The young princess, you may be sure, was not long in giving her consent, and as they spoke, a splendid carriage drove up. It was driven by eight beautiful horses decked with plumes of feathers and a golden harness, and behind rode the prince's servant, the faithful Henry, who had bewailed the misfortune of his dear master so long and bitterly that his heart had well-nigh burst. Then all set out full of joy for the prince's kingdom, where they arrived safely and lived happily a great many years.

The Runaway Bunny

By Margaret Wise Brown

Once there was a little bunny who wanted to run away. So he said to his mother, "I am running away."

"If you run away," said his mother, "I will run after you. For you are my little bunny."

"If you run after me," said the little bunny, "I will become a fish in a trout stream and I will swim away from you."

"If you become a fish in a trout stream," said his mother, "I will become a fisherman and I will fish for you."

"If you become a fisherman," said the little bunny, "I will become a rock on the mountain high above you."

"If you become a rock on the mountain high above me," said his mother, "I will be a mountain climber, and I will climb to where you are."

"If you become a mountain climber," said the little bunny, "I will be a crocus in a hidden garden."

"If you become a crocus in a hidden garden," said his mother, "I will be a gardener. And I will find you."

"If you are a gardener and find me," said the little bunny, "I will be a bird and fly away from you."

"If you become a bird and fly away from me," said his mother, "I will be a tree that you come home to."

"If you become a tree," said the little bunny, "I will become a little sailboat, and I will sail away from you."

"If you become a sailboat and sail away from me," said his mother, "I will become the wind and blow you where I want you to go."

"If you become the wind and blow me," said the little bunny, "I will join the circus and fly away on a flying trapeze."

"If you go flying on a flying trapeze," said his mother, "I will be a tightrope walker, and I will walk across the air to you."

"If you become a tightrope walker and walk across the air," said the bunny, "I will become a little boy and run into the house."

"If you become a little boy and run into a house," said the mother bunny, "I will become your mother and catch you in my arms and hug you."

"Shucks," said the bunny, "I might just as well stay where I am and be your little bunny."

And so he did.

"Have a carrot," said the mother bunny.

Goldilocks & the Three Bears

By Robert Southey

Once upon a time, there lived in a pretty little house in the midst of a great forest three bears. The first was a Big Bear, with a big head, big paws, and a big gruff voice.

The second was a Middling-Sized Bear, with a middling-sized head, a middling-sized body, and a voice that was neither very loud nor very soft.

The third was a wee little Baby Bear, with a wee little head, a wee little body, and a teeny-weeny voice between a whine and a squeak.

Now although the home of these three bears was rather rough, they had in it all the things they wanted. There was a big chair for the Big Bear to sit in, a big porridge-bowl from which he could eat his breakfast, and a big bed, very strongly made, on which he could sleep at night. The Middling-Sized Bear had a middling-sized porridge-bowl, with a chair and a bed to match. For the Little Bear there was a nice little chair, a neat little bed, and a porridge-bowl that held just enough to satisfy a little bear's appetite.

Near the house of the three bears lived a child whose name was Goldilocks. She was very pretty, with long curls of the brightest gold that shone and glittered in the sunshine. She was round and plump, merry and light-hearted, always running and jumping about and singing the whole day long. When Goldilocks laughed, her laugh rang out with a clear silvery sound that was very pleasant to hear.

One day she ran off into the woods to gather flowers. When she had gone some way, she began to make wreathes and garlands of wild roses and honeysuckle, and scarcely thought at all of where she was going or of how she was to get back.

At last she came to a part of the forest where there was an open space in which no trees grew. There was a kind of pathway trampled or stamped across it, as if someone with broad heavy feet was used to walking there.

Following this for a short distance, she came, much to her surprise, to a funny little house roughly made of wood.

There was a small keyhole in the door of the house and Goldilocks peeped through to see if anyone was at home. She strained her eyes till they ached; but the house seemed quite empty.

The longer she peeped, the more she wanted to know who lived in this funny little house and what kind of people they were; and, if the truth must be told, a good many other girls would have been quite as inquisitive.

At last her wish to see the inside of the house became so strong that she could resist no longer: there seemed to be someone pushing her forward, while a voice called in her ear, "Go in, Goldilocks, go in." So, after a little more peeping, she opened the door very softly, and timidly walked right in.

But where were the bears at this time? And why were they not there to welcome their pretty little guest?

Every morning they used to get up early—wise bears as they were—and when the Middling-Sized Bear, who was also the Mummy Bear, had cooked the porridge she would say, if it was a fine morning: "The porridge is too hot just yet. We will go for a little walk, my dears, the fresh air will give us an appetite, and when we come back the porridge will be just right." And that is why the bears were not at home when Goldilocks walked into their house.

When she came into the bears' room, Goldilocks was surprised to see a big porridge bowl, a middling-sized porridge-bowl, and a little porridge-bowl all standing on the table.

"Some of the people who live here must eat a good deal more than the others," she thought. "Whoever can want all the porridge that is in the big bowl? It looks very good. I wonder whether it is sweetened with sugar, or if they put salt into it. I'll just try a taste."

So she put the great spoon into the big bowl and ladled out some of the Big Bear's breakfast.

Now there was so much porridge in the Big Bear's bowl that it kept hot longer than the porridge in the middling-sized bowl and in the little bowl. When Goldilocks put the big spoon in her mouth, she drew back with a scream and danced with pain. For the porridge was very, very hot and burned her mouth, and Goldilocks did not like it at all.

"Whatever sort of person can eat such stuff?" she said.

So she tried the middling-sized bowl; and you may be sure she took good care to blow on the spoon before it went in her mouth. But she need not have been so careful, for the porridge was quite cold and sticky. So she stuck the spoon upright in the bowl and wondered again whoever could eat such stuff.

Then she tried the little porridge; and the porridge in that was just right, neither too hot, nor too cold, and with just the right quantity of sugar.

Having finished the first spoonful, Goldilocks thought she would try a second; and then, being still hungry, she had a third and a fourth and a fifth. By this time she could see the bottom of the bowl, so she thought she might as well look round for a comfortable chair in which to sit and finish all that was left.

First she scrambled up into the Big Bear's chair. It was cold and hard and much too high for her. Next she tried the Middling-Sized Bear's chair, but that was just as bad the other way, too soft and bulging.

Then she caught sight of the teeny-tiny chair that belonged to the Little Bear. It cracked beneath her weight, but was just as comfy as ever a chair could be. So she sat in it and finished up the very last spoonful of porridge.

Then she began to feel very tired and sleepy and gave a great yawn. There was a crack, a groan, and a crash! and down went the bottom of the chair, for you see it was only made for a wee little bear to sit in.

Goldilocks felt a little frightened when she found herself on the floor but soon got up, and, still being very sleepy, thought she would go upstairs and see if there was a bed to lie on.

She looked at the beds to see which she should rest upon and tried the big bed first. It would not do at all—the pillow was hard and so big that it kept her head too high. The middling-sized bed was no better—it was so soft that she flopped right down in it. Then, Goldilocks tried the little bed and that was just right—sweet and dainty, very white and very soft, with snowy sheets, and a pillow exactly the right height. So Goldilocks laid herself down, with her pretty head on the comfy pillow, and in a few seconds fell asleep.

But before she dropped off to sleep, Goldilocks wondered a little what the people of the house, who owned the porridge-bowls, and the chairs, and the beds, would say if they knew she was there and what she had done.

Soon—very soon—there were sounds into the room below. A big heavy foot went bump—bump—bump; a middling-sized foot went tramp—tramp—tramp; and a tiny little foot went pit-pat—pit-pat—pit-pat. The three bears had come home to breakfast! And directly as they came into the room, they all three sniffed and sniffed and sniffed.

When the Big Bear came to his porridge-bowl, and found the spoon sticking upright, he knew at once that someone had meddled with it. So he gave an angry

roar and growled in his big voice: "SOMEBODY HAS BEEN AT MY PORRIDGE!"

At this the Middling-Sized Bear ran across the room to look at her breakfast; and when she found the spoon sticking up in her porridge-bowl, she cried out, though not so loudly as the Big Bear had done: "SOMEBODY HAS BEEN AT MY PORRIDGE!"

Then the Little Bear ran to his porridge-bowl; and when he found all his porridge gone, and not even enough left for the spoon to stand upright in, he squeaked in a poor piteous little voice: "Somebody has been at my porridge and has eaten it all up!"

He tilted up his little porridge-bowl to show the others, stuffed his little forepaws into his little eyes, and began to cry.

While the Little Bear cried, Big Bear looked around and caught sight of his chair, on which Goldilocks had left the cushion all awry. This made him angrier still, and he growled: "SOMEBODY HAS BEEN SITTING IN MY CHAIR!" Then the Middling-Sized Bear noticed that in the soft cushion of her chair was a hollow where Goldilocks had sat down. So she called out in her middling-sized voice: "SOME-BODY HAS BEEN SITTING IN MY CHAIR!"

The Little Bear stopped crying for a moment and looked at his chair. Then he forgot all about the porridge and called out in his squeaky little voice: "Somebody has been sitting in my chair and has pushed the bottom out of it!"

The three Bears all looked at one another in surprise. Whoever could have dared to do such things—in their house too!

"Some mortal has been here," said the Big Bear.

"Yes," said the Middling-Sized Bear, sniffing around.

"Let's go upstairs."

So the Big Bear went stumping up the stairs, with the Middling-Sized Bear at his heels and the Little Bear last of all.

Goldilocks had tumbled the Big Bear's bolster in trying to make it low enough for her head. The Big Bear noticed it at once and growled: "SOMEBODY HAS BEEN LYING IN MY BED!"

And the Middling-Sized Bear said in her middling-sized voice: "SOMEBODY HAS BEEN LYING IN MY BED!"

The Little Bear saw something that made the hair on his body stand on end.

There was the bed, all smooth and white; the counterpane was in its place and the pillow too; but on them, fast asleep, lay little Goldilocks. To make quite sure, he climbed on the end of the bed and looked over the rail. Then: "Somebody has been lying on my bed!" squealed the Little Bear, "and she's lying on it still!"

The Big Bear, the Middling-Sized Bear, and the Little Bear all stood with their mouths wide open, staring in surprise at Goldilocks. Then the Big Bear gave a grunt; and the Middling-Sized Bear gave a growl; and the Little Bear, who loved his

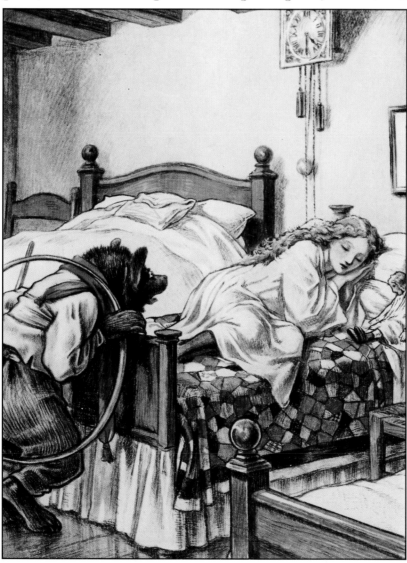

little bed very much because it was so comfy, cried and cried and cried, and thought perhaps he would never be able to sleep on it anymore.

Now when the Big Bear spoke, Goldilocks dreamed of a thunderstorm; and when the Middling-Sized Bear spoke, she dreamed that the wind was making the roses nod. But when she heard the little, small, wee voice of the Little, Small, Wee Bear, it was so sharp and so shrill that it awakened her at once. Up she started; and when she

saw the Three Bears on one side of the bed, she tumbled herself out at the other and ran to the window. Now the window was open, because the Bears, like good, tidy Bears, as they were, always opened their bedchamber window when they got up in the morning. Out Goldilocks jumped into the garden.

Then she ran through the woods as fast as she could and never stopped till she reached home.

And you may be sure she never went wandering into the wood again, so the Big Bear and the Middling-Sized Bear and the Little Bear ate their porridge in peace all the rest of their days.

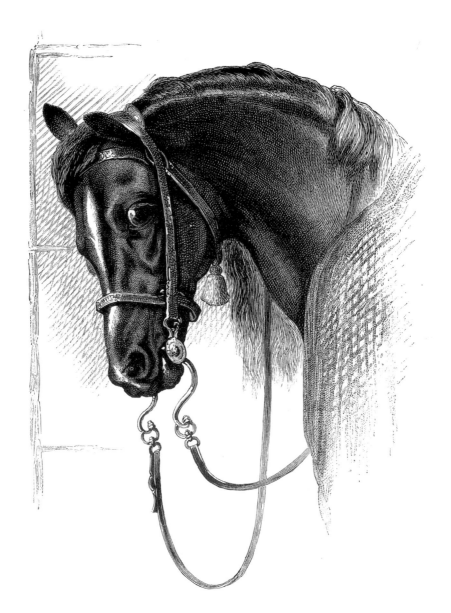

Black Beauty

(A Stormy Day passage)

By Anna Sewell

One day late in the autumn, my master had a long journey to go on business. I was put into the dogcart, and John went with his master. I always liked to go in the dogcart; it was so light, and the high wheels ran along so pleasantly. There had been a great deal of rain, and now the wind was very high and blew the dry leaves across the road in a shower. We went along merrily till we came to the toll bar and the low wooden bridge. The riverbanks were rather high, and the bridge, instead of rising, went across just level, so that in the middle, if the river was full, the water would be nearly up to the woodwork and planks; but as there were good substantial rails on each side, people did not mind it.

The man at the gate said the river was rising fast, and he feared it would be a bad night. Many of the meadows were under water, and in one low part of the road the water was halfway up to my knees; the bottom was good, and the master drove gently, so it was no matter.

When we got to the town, of course, I had a good bait, but as the master's business engaged him a long time, we did not start for home till rather late in the afternoon. The wind was then much higher, and I heard the master say to John that he had never been out in such a storm; and so I thought, as we went along the skirts of a wood, where the great branches were swaying about like twigs, and the rushing sound was terrible.

"I wish we were well out of this wood," said my master.

"Yes, sir," said John, "it would be rather awkward if one of these branches came down upon us."

The words were scarcely out of his mouth, when there was a groan, and a crack, and a splitting sound, and tearing, crashing down amongst the other trees came an oak, torn up by the roots, and fell right across the road just before us. I will never say I was not frightened, for I was. I stopped still, and I believe I trembled; of course, I did not turn round or run away; I was not brought up to that. John jumped out and was in a moment at my head.

"That was a very near touch," said my master. "What's to be done now?"

"Well, sir, we can't drive over that tree, nor yet get round it; there will be nothing for it but to go back to the four crossways, and that will be a good six miles before we get round to the wooden bridge again; it will make us late, but the horse is fresh."

So back we went and round by the crossroads; but by the time we got to the bridge it was very nearly dark; we could just see that the water was over the middle of it; but as that happened sometimes when the floods were out, master did not stop. We were going along at a good pace, but the moment my feet touched the first part of the bridge, I felt sure there was something wrong. I dare not go forward, and I made a dead stop. "Go on, Beauty," said my master, and he gave me a touch with the whip, but I dare not stir; he gave me a sharp cut; I jumped, but I dare not go forward.

"There's something wrong, sir," said John, and he sprang out of the dogcart and came to my head and looked all about. He tried to lead me forward. "Come on, Beauty, what's the matter?" Of course I could not tell him, but I knew very well that the bridge was not safe.

Just then the man at the toll-gate on the other side ran out of the house, tossing a torch about like one mad..

"Hoy, hoy, hoy! halloo! stop!" he cried.

"What's the matter?" shouted my master.

"The bridge is broken in the middle and part of it is carried away; if you come on you'll be into the river."

"Thank God!" said my master. "You Beauty!" said John and took the bridle and gently turned me round to the right-hand road by the riverside. The sun had set some time; the wind seemed to have lulled off after that furious blast which tore up the tree. It grew darker and darker, stiller and stiller. I trotted quietly along, the wheels hardly making a sound on the soft road. For a good long while neither master nor John spoke, and then master began in a serious voice. I could not understand much of what they said, but I found they thought, if I had gone on as the master wanted me, most likely the bridge would have given way under us, and horse, chaise, master, and man would have fallen into the river; and as the current was flowing very strongly, and there was no light and no help at hand, it was more than likely we would have been drowned. Master said, God had given men reason, by which they could find out things for themselves; but He had given animals knowledge which did not depend on reason, and which was much more prompt and perfect in its way, and by which they had often saved the lives of men. John had many stories to tell of dogs and horses and the wonderful things they had done; he thought people did not value their animals half enough, nor make friends of them as they ought to do. I am sure he makes friends of them if ever a man did.

At last we came to the Park gates and found the gardener looking out for us. He said that mistress had been in a dreadful way ever since dark, fearing some accident had happened, and that she had sent James off on Justice, the roan cob, toward the wooden bridge to make inquiry after us.

We saw a light at the hall door and at the upper windows, and as we came up mistress ran out, saying, "Are you really safe, my dear? Oh! I have been so anxious, fancying all sorts of things. Have you had no accident?"

"No, my dear; but if your Black Beauty had not been wiser than we were, we should all have been carried down the river at the wooden bridge." I heard no more, as they went into the house, and John took me to the stable. Oh, what a good supper he gave me that night, a good bran mash and some crushed beans with my oats, and such a thick bed of straw! and I was glad of it, for I was tired.

Lions and Tigers and Bears

From the movie *The Wizard of Oz*

Lions and Tigers and Bears, oh my!
Lions and Tigers and Bears, oh my!
Lions and Tigers and Bears, oh my!
LIONS! AND TIGERS! AND BEARS!
OH MY!

The Ugly Duckling

By Hans Christian Andersen

The hay was stacked in the meadows, the wheat was golden, and the oats were still green. It was summer. By the side of an old mansion was a stream. There bulrushes grew higher than a child's head, and in the pleasant shade of the rushes was a Mother Duck sitting on her nest of eggs. Often she grew very tired and lonesome. The other ducks cared more about swimming in the center of the stream than about gossiping with her among the bulrushes.

At last, on a sunny morning, one of the eggs cracked. With a "cheep, cheep," out came a downy duckling. Soon the other eggs cracked also, and around the Mother Duck were five little ones.

"How large the world is!" they cried.

"Did you think," quacked the Mother Duck, "that the world was as small as the inside of an egg? Why it reaches across the stream and over to the Parson's meadows, but I have never been that far."

"Are they all here?" asked an Old Duck who came to call.

"All I think," answered the Mother Duck, "and never have I had so fine a family." She got up from the nest, and then saw there was still one large egg remaining.

"That," said the Old Duck, "that is no egg from our nests! Leave it where it is."

"Since I have taken so much trouble," said the Mother Duck, "I'll wait until Midsummer Fair," and she returned to her nest.

The Mother Duck continued to sit on the nest, and finally, on the afternoon of Midsummer Fair, the large egg cracked and out came a large, gray-feathered creature, quite unlike the other ducklings.

"That," said the Old Duck, who had come to gossip again, "that is certainly no duckling, whatever else it may be. A homelier being I never beheld."

"Well," answered the Mother Duck, "tomorrow we'll see."

The next morning the Mother Duck called her ducklings and the gray one to her and took them to the pond. At first they went under the water, then they came quickly to the top. Their legs seemed to work by themselves. How delightful it was to be moving through the water! And the big gray one swam even better than the rest. He was very strong.

"He," said the Mother Duck, "is certainly none of mine. Young ducklings never venture so far."

When they reached the center of the stream, there was a great commotion. All the ducks were quarreling over an eel's head.

"Ah," said the Mother Duck, "that is the way of the world!"

When the ducks saw the ducklings, they all exclaimed, "Why, what a fine family you have! But that biggest one, how ugly he is! He looks as if he ought to be made over again."

"That cannot be done," said the Mother Duck. "He is big and strong, and he is sure to make his way in the world."

Just then a large drake bit the big Duckling on the neck. Others began to strike at him. Even his brothers and sisters pecked at the poor creature because he was so homely.

"Go away, you are different from us," they cried.

As the Duckling grew older and bigger, even the Mother Duck drove him away, and the maid who fed the ducks kicked at him whenever he tried to join the others.

One day, half running, half flying, the Ugly Duckling got over the farmyard fence, hoping to leave his tormentors behind. He came to a large pond where wild ducks gathered.

"Mercy," they cried, "how strange you are. But come, be a free creature and fly with us. We do not care how you look if only you do not marry into our families."

Just then there came a loud bang, bang, bang. The smell of powder filled the air. Hunters were near. Away flew the wild ducks. Close to the Ugly Duckling came a great, hairy creature with a long red tongue. The Duckling could feel its hot breath stir its feathers. But the dog did not touch him.

"There's one good thing about being so frightful. Even the dogs will not come near," thought the Ugly Duckling. It was evening before the Duckling dared stir from the rushes. Then he flapped his way across the fields. As he did so, small birds rose from the grasses with shrill cries of alarm. "The very birds fly away at the sight of me," he thought.

At last he came to a small rickety hut. The only thing which kept it upright was that it seemed not to know which way to fall. There lived an Old Woman, her Cat, and a Hen whom she loved as though it had been her child. The Ugly Duckling went inside.

"This may indeed be good fortune," said the Old Woman, and she let the Duckling stay and eat the crumbs dropped by the Hen.

"How ugly you are," said the Cat.

"No fine feathers like mine," said the Hen.

"Can you purr like me?" asked the Cat. "Can you send sparks from your tail?"

The Duckling shook his head.

"Stupid. Can you lay eggs like me?" asked the Hen. "Useless one, can you bake bread like the Old Woman?

This also the Duckling could not do.

"Then, pray tell, of what use are you in this world?"

"I can swim," said the Duckling. "How good it is to dive under the water!"

"Water!" squeaked the Hen.

"Swim!" cried the Cat.

"The Old Woman does not like the water. I, the Hen, do not wish to swim, nor the Cat to dive. Surely you must be mad!" The Hen preened her feathers angrily.

"You do not understand me," said the Duckling.

"We do not understand you!" The Cat licked her front paw. "The Old Woman is the cleverest one for miles about. The Hen is known for her wisdom. And as for me, I am no fool. If we do not understand you, it is clear that you are wrong and we are right."

This the Duckling did not quite believe, but he said nothing. As the days passed, the Duckling longed more and more for the cool, rippling waves of the pond. And since he had no peace day or night, he left the hut and returned to the water.

Soon the leaves on the trees fell to the ground, brown and yellow. Frost touched the meadows. A black raven in a nearby tree called out, "Caw, caw." The very sound sent shivers of cold beneath the feathers of the Duckling. It was fall.

One morning, as the sun shone brightly, a flock of dazzling white birds flew above him like snowy clouds against a blue sky. They were wild swans, and they uttered a strange loud cry as they flew.

The Duckling rose from the water and then answered them with a call like their own. When they were gone, the Duckling dreamed of them, but their beauty served only to make him seem uglier and more misshapen.

Colder and colder grew the days, more bitter the nights. Now the Duckling was quite alone. All the other ducks and birds had flown south or were snug in their coops. Ice formed on the edge of the pond. Snow fell. The Duckling had to swim faster and faster so as not to be trapped by the ice.

One morning he was so weary he could swim no longer. He was caught fast in the ice near the center of the pond. He closed his eyes. "This," he thought, "will be the end."

A farmer walking home from his work saw the Duckling frozen in the center of the pond. With an ax he broke the ice and took the Duckling home to his children. The children ran toward him with cries of delight. They wanted to play with their new pet. But the Duckling, who had known nothing but ill-treatment, was terrified. He flew into the milk pan. The farmer's wife went after him with the tongs. Next he fell into the butter crock and from there into the meal tub. The door happened to be open and he ran out into the frozen garden. How miserable he was!

Each day of the long winter was more terrible than the rest. When at last the warm sun returned, and the larks sang high above the world, he stretched his wings, surprised to find that he had lived through the time of blackness.

As he flew, his wings made a whir, whir, so strong were they. He came to a garden through which ran a gentle stream. Flowers bloomed on either side. Fruit trees were fragrant with pink-tipped blossoms, and lilacs swayed in the breeze. As he entered the garden, swimming slowly in the stream, he saw coming toward him three majestic white swans. Their feathers gleamed in the sunlight. They floated on the blue water like white clouds in the sky.

"Ah," thought the Duckling, "they will surely kill me, because I am so hideous. But it is better to be killed by these beings from paradise than to be pecked by the ducks, chased by the cat, and kicked by the kitchen maid."

He bent his head and waited. There in the clear water he saw his own form mirrored—a long graceful neck, feathers whiter than winter frost. How he had changed since he last saw his reflection in the water! He, himself, was a swan!

The three birds came to greet him and stroked him with their beaks. The children in the garden called out, "Oh, see, here is a new one! He is more beautiful than any other!"

They threw bread and bits of cake for him to eat.

The days were warm and golden. Because he had known such sorrow, the Duckling's joy was now the greater. "It does not matter how ugly you are," he thought, "if you are born from a swan's egg."

Each hour now was happier than the last. He rustled his feathers and raised his slender neck. "I never dared dream of such happiness when I was the Ugly Duckling."

Milk-White Moon, Put the Cows to Sleep

By Carl Sandburg

Milk-white moon, put the cows to sleep,
Since five o'clock in the morning,
Since they stood up out of the grass,
Where they slept on their knees and hocks,
They have eaten grass and given their milk
And eaten grass again and given milk.
And kept their heads and teeth at the earth's face.

Now they are looking at you, milk-white moon.
Carelessly as they look at the level landscapes,
Carelessly as they look at a pail of new white milk,
They are looking at you, wondering not at all, at all,
If the moon is the skim face top of a pail of milk,
Wondering not at all, carelessly looking.
Put the cows to sleep, milk-white moon,
Put the cows to sleep.

The Owl and the Pussycat

By Edward Lear

The Owl and the Pussycat went to sea
In a beautiful pea-green boat;
They took some honey, and plenty of money,
Wrapped up in a five-pound note.

The Owl looked up to the stars above,
And sang to a small guitar,
"O lovely Pussy! O Pussy, my love,
What a beautiful Pussy you are,
You are,
You are!
What a beautiful Pussy you are!"

Pussy said to the Owl, "You elegant fowl,
How charmingly sweet you sing!
O let us be married! Too long we have tarried:
But what shall we do for a ring?"

They sailed away, for a year and a day,
To the land where the Bong-tree grows;
And there in a wood a Piggy-wig stood
With a ring at the end of his nose,
His nose,
His nose,
With a ring at the end of his nose.

"Dear Pig, are you willing to sell for one shilling
Your ring?" Said the Piggy, "I will."
So they took it away, and were married next day
By the Turkey who lives on the hill.

They dined on mince and slices of quince,
Which they ate with a runcible spoon;
And hand in hand, on the edge of the sand,
They danced by the light of the moon,
The moon,
The moon,
They danced by the light of the moon.

Chicken Little

Anonymous

One morning, an acorn fell on Chicken Little's head. PLOP! Chicken Little looked up. "The sky is falling," he cheeped. I must tell the king!"

"Hello," clucked Henny Penny. "Where are you going in such a hurry?"

"The sky is falling," cheeped Chicken Little, "and I must tell the king."

"Then I will trot with you," clucked Henny Penny

So off they went.

And they went along, and they went along, and they went along.

"Hello," crowed Cocky Locky. "Where are you going in such a hurry?"

"The sky is falling," cheeped Chicken Little, "and I must tell the king."

"Then I will strut with you," crowed Cocky Locky.

So off they went.

And they went along, and they went along, and they went along.

"Hello," quacked Ducky Lucky. "Where are you going in such a hurry?"

"The sky is falling," cheeped Chicken Little, "and I must tell the king."

"Then I will waddle with you," quacked Ducky Lucky. So off they went.

And they went along, and they went along, and they went along.

"Hello," gaggled Drakey Lakey. "Where are you going in such a hurry?"

"The sky is falling," cheeped Chicken Little, "and I must tell the king."

"Then I will toddle with you," gaggled Drakey Lakey. So off they went.

And they went along, and they went along, and they went along.

"Hello," honked Goosey Loosey. "Where are you going in such a hurry?"

"The sky is falling," cheeped Chicken Little, "and I must tell the king."

"Then I will jog with you," honked Goosey Loosey. So off they went.

And they went along, and they went along, and they went along.

"Hello," gobbled Turkey Lurkey. "Where are you going in such a hurry?"

"The sky is falling," cheeped Chicken Little, "and I must tell the king."

"Then I will march with you," gobbled Turkey Lurkey. So off they went.

And they went along, and they went along, and they went along.

"Hello," growled Foxy Loxy. "Where are you going in such a hurry?"

"The sky is falling," cheeped Chicken Little, "and I must tell the king."

"Come with me," growled Foxy Loxy. "I'll take you to the king."

So Chicken Little, Henny Penny, Cocky Locky, Ducky Lucky, Drakey Lakey, Goosey Loosey, and Turkey Lurkey followed Foxy Loxy straight into his lair—and never came out again.

And Chicken Little never told the king the sky was falling.

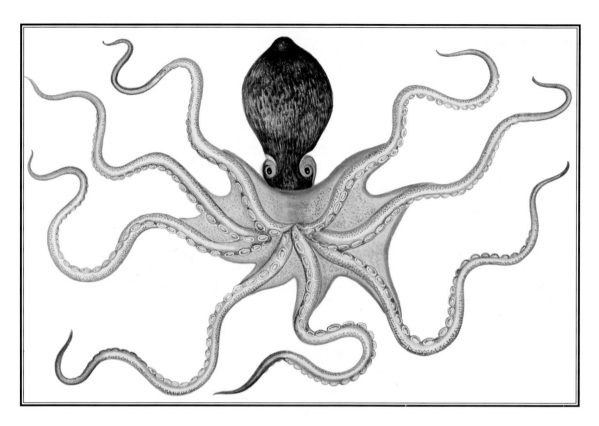

Octopus's Garden

By Richard Starkey

I'd like to be under the sea
In an Octopus's Garden in the shade.
He'd let us in, knows where we've been
In his Octopus's Garden in the shade.
I'd ask my friends to come and see
An Octopus's Garden with me:
I'd like to be under the sea
In an Octopus's Garden in the shade.

We would be warm below the storm
In our little hideaway beneath the waves.
Resting our head on the sea bed
In an Octopus's Garden near a cave.
We would sing and dance around
Because we know we can't be found.
I'd like to be under the sea
In an Octopus's Garden in the shade.

We would shout and swim about
The coral that lies beneath the waves.
Oh, what joy for every girl and boy
Knowing they're happy and they're safe.
We would be so happy, you and me.
No one there to tell us what to do.
I'd like to be under the sea
In an Octopus's Garden with you.

The Prince, the Tways, the Magpie and the Cats

By Maude Adams

The Prince with his Tways
In an emerald cage,
The Magpie holding a note,
In the Cats' round eyes.

The Cats are giving,
All these Moon-watchers,
A little break this evening.

I Saw a Peacock

Anonymous

I saw a peacock with a fiery tail,
I saw a tiny ant swallow up a whale.
I saw wild eyes all flaming fire,
I saw a house bigger than the moon and higher.
I saw the sun at twelve o'clock at night,
I saw the man that saw this wondrous sight.

Little Bo Peep

By Mother Goose

Little Bo Peep has lost her sheep,
And can't tell where to find them;
Leave them alone, and they'll come home,
And bring their tails behind them.

The Animal Fair

Anonymous

I went to the Animal Fair,
The birds and the bees were there.
The big baboon,
By the light of the moon,
Was combing his auburn hair.

Andy Panda

Anonymous

Andy Panda was the handiest little panda you could ever wish to meet. If there was anything to be mended, Andy mended it.

There was one time when he mended a grandfather's clock for his Grandfather—why he mended it so well that afterwards he had enough pieces left over to make with a few more old bits of wood and string—a glider.

"I am going to take it up on the roof and try it out," he told his friend Claud Chimp. "I believe in this grand invention because, Claud, everyone knows how it's been proven that TIME FLIES!"

Three Blind Mice

By Mother Goose

Three blind mice,
See how they run!
They all ran after the farmer's wife,
Who cut off their tails with a carving knife.
Did you ever see such a sight in your life
As three blind mice?

Acknowledgments

We wish to thank the following properties, whose cooperation has made this unique collection possible. All care has been taken to trace ownership of these selections and to make a full acknowledgment. If any errors or omissions have occured, they will be corrected in subsequent editions, provided notification is sent to the compiler.

Front Cover   Eulalie, from *Eight Nursery Tales*, 1932.

Front Flap   Anonymous, from *The Children's Big Storybook*, 1928.

Endpapers   Kimi Ga Yo, 1925.

Title   Anonymous, *Cat and the Fiddle*, n.d.

Title Spot   Anonymous scrap, n.d.

Copyright Spot   Francis Kirn, from *Annual Mammoth Book*, 1946.

Preface   Anonymous, *The Nursery*, 1877.

Contents   T. Thirkell Pearce, from *Animal Fun*, n.d.

11   Millicent Sowerby, from *Alice's Adventures in Wonderland*, 1907.

12   John Durand, *Mary Beekman, about Two Years Old*, 1766.

14   Albrecht Dürer, *The Brown Witch*, 1502.

15   M. Boutet de Monvel, from *Filles et Garcons*, 1906.

16   Milo Winter, from *The Aesop for Children*, 1919.

18   Anonymous, from *The Nursery*, 1877.

19   E. Boyd Smith, from *The E. Boyd Smith Mother Goose*, 1919.

21   Utagawa Hiroshige, *Mikawa Island, Kanasugi, and Minowa*, 1857.

22   Studley Burroughs, from *Science Stories, Book One*, 1933.

23   Corrine Malvern, from *Storytime Tales*, circa 1948.

24   C. Cole Phillips, n.d.

25   John R. Neil, n.d.

25 Spot Palmer Cox, n.d.

26   Ernest H. Shepard, from *The Wind in the Willows*, 1908

29   Ernest H. Shepard, from *The Wind in the Willows*, 1908

30   Ernest H. Shepard, from *The Wind in the Willows*, 1908

31   Edward Julius Detmold, from *The Fables of Aesop*, 1909.